GUCCI GIRLS

CUTTING IT

FASHION RETAIL
ACADEMY

Library

Renewals: 020 7307 2365

Email: library@fra.ac.uk

15 Gresse Street, London W1T

00001299

To Kate and Eve,
the original Gucci girls!

SIMON AND SCHUSTER

First published in Great Britain by Simon & Schuster UK Ltd, 2005
A Viacom company

1 3 5 7 9 10 8 6 4 2

Simon & Schuster UK Ltd
Africa House
64-78 Kingsway
London WC2B 6AH

A CIP catalogue record for this book is available from the British Library

ISBN 0 689 87288 7

Typeset by SX Composing DTP, Rayleigh, Essex
Printed and bound in Great Britain
by Cox & Wyman Ltd, Reading, Berkshire

www.simonsays.co.uk

ONE

I can do this stuff! Marina told herself. *I can, I can!*

Naked man alert! Frankie took a deep breath. *Whoah, naked man!*

The life model walked into the centre of the studio and took off his robe.

What's the big deal? Sinead thought. She chose a chunky stick of charcoal from her box.

The scrawny guy sat on a chair. His skin was the colour of cheese, his light-brown hair matted into long dreads.

'Billy's body has good definition, so make the most of it,' the tutor advised. 'You're using A1 paper, and I want your drawing to fill the whole area.'

Jeez! Frankie breathed out. Man, this life-

1

drawing deal was in your face. Was she the only one here who was finding it weird? She looked over at the girl with long, blonde hair on her left.

Marina swallowed hard and tried not to feel nauseous. She picked up the messy stick of charcoal and twiddled it between her tapered fingers, blood-red fingernails stark against the black.

The model was stretched out full-frontal now.

'Yes, that's right.' Jack Irvine, the tutor, nodded as Sinead used the side of her charcoal block to shade in the dark areas. 'Don't hold back,' he told the others. 'I know this is a first for most of you, but you're not schoolkids any more. This is the Central School of Fashion and you're *bona fide* students now, so grow up and concentrate on your technique.'

Suitably chastised, Frankie blinked and forced herself to start work.

'Gross!' Marina groaned. After the ordeal of the life-drawing class, she, Frankie and Sinead had sloped off for coffee. 'What was that model guy thinking? He must have been at least sixty years old!'

'Yeah, you'd have to pay me shed-loads to do that,' Frankie agreed. 'I mean, getting your kit off in front of a room full of strangers for just twenty quid – it's not worth the shame!'

'It's a job,' Sinead pointed out. 'Better than stacking supermarket shelves.'

'No way!' Frankie and Marina argued. Personally, they would take piling up baked-bean cans over nude modelling any day.

'Anyway, listen to the good Catholic girl! What would your mama think?' Marina stirred her black coffee and winked at Sinead, before checking out the room. There were two other refugees from the life class, plus two guys she'd seen somewhere before. Freshers' Week? Serving behind the Union bar? No, she couldn't remember where. She gave up and checked her reflection in the mirror behind the counter.

'Did you notice he went to sleep on the job?' Frankie said, grinning, her voice almost drowned out by the hiss and suck of the coffee machine.

The others laughed.

'No, not like that! I mean, he got paid for taking a snooze.'

'And he moved,' Marina complained. 'I had to rub his torso out and start over.' She giggled. The two guys across the room were looking their way and muttering.

Frankie leaned back and eased her hands over her flat stomach. 'I kept wanting to laugh so much it hurt!'

'Haven't either of you two *seen* a naked man before?' Sinead muttered.

'Ye-ah, of course!' Marina said, edgily.

Frankie kept quiet. Then she changed the subject. 'Your drawing was cool,' she told Sinead.

'Hey, don't look now, but where have we seen those two guys before?' Marina asked, in a big stage whisper.

Sinead and Frankie turned to stare.

'I *said*, don't look!' Marina hissed.

The one in the leather jacket was getting up and coming towards them. No, he wasn't. He was heading to the counter for more coffee. The other, more hunky, one was reading a music magazine.

4

'They live in a house across the square from us,' Frankie told Marina, matter-of-factly. 'The one in the jacket rides a silver motorbike. I've seen him parking it outside.'

'He's cute,' Marina said.

'You two together would be like Beauty and the Beast,' Sinead said. Marina looked like she'd walked out of a nineteen-forties movie – blonde hair, painted nails, gloss-slicked lips – while the Neanderthal biker guy probably lived in a cave and communicated in grunts. Except that Frankie had just said he lived in the house opposite them. 'Now, the one reading the magazine – *he's* cute!'

'More coffee anyone?' Marina said suddenly, jumping up and heading for the counter. Before you could say 'Marilyn Monroe', she was deep in conversation with Leather-Jacket Man.

'I'm a first-year fashion student here at Central,' Marina cooed.

'Yeah?' Rob paid for his coffee.

'You look like Marlon Brando,' she told him, out of the blue.

He laughed. 'Yeah, in *The Godfather*.'

'No, Brando like he was in *On the Waterfront*. Y'know: "I could've been a contender!"' *All muscles and six-pack and sexy voice*, she thought to herself. 'I'm Marina. We live near you on Walgrave Square.'

'Rob,' he told her, taking his change. 'Which number?'

'His name's Rob and he lives at Number 45,' Marina reported to Sinead and Frankie three minutes later. 'And guess what? He works in the jewellery lab!'

'Where?' Frankie asked. Jewellery was her thing.

'Here, at college,' Marina explained. Then she held up her phone. 'And I got his number!'

'Two-nil to Arsenal,' Rob said. He was slouched on the sofa back at his place, boots and jacket unzipped.

'Cool,' Travis murmured, his back to the television, sitting at the table and reading up about his expensive new camera lens.

Rob threw a cold can across the room. 'Fancy a lager?'

'Cool, thanks.'

Pssst-pssst! The magical, musical chorus of two cans opening in unison.

'Only three minutes to go, not including extra time,' Rob reported. 'Hey, did you see that blonde chatting me up in the coffee bar?'

'No, mate. When?' The lens was an up-to-the-minute telephoto and had cost Travis an arm and a leg.

'Earlier. A fresher. She asked for my number.'

'In your dreams.'

'She bloody did.' The match went into extra time. The Gunners had it sewn up now.

Travis fitted the new lens onto his Nikon, then zoomed in on Rob slumped on the sofa. 'Yeah, right – and you're God's gift to women!'

Rob grinned. 'The first years always fancy an older man, mate. Whoah, ref, your effing man's offside!'

Rob was caught in the viewfinder now, a can of lager in hand, leaning towards the television and swearing his head off. Travis zoomed out and focused on the screen instead. 'It must be a wind-up,' he muttered.

'Nope,' Rob promised confidently. The match ended and he relaxed. 'Her name's Marina. She said she'd call me.'

It's all so . . . new! Frankie thought, as she and Marina stood on the doorstep waiting for Sinead to find her key. New house, new city, new people. She'd been here a week, sussed out the charity shops and market stalls selling vintage gear, done the freshers' stuff, got drunk, and joined about fifty societies and clubs, but she still felt like Gretel lost in the woods without Hansel. It was dark, there were big bad wolves and woodcutters out there.

'Get a move on, Sinead, it's freezing!' Marina moaned.

'Wear a jacket,' Sinead suggested, turfing out half a dozen lip-glosses, a hairbrush, some coins and paper tissues from her bag.

How come the other two act like they've been at college for ever? Frankie wondered. She was in awe, totally overwhelmed.

'Hey, come and see your hot new date!' Travis called Rob away from the post-match analysis.

He stood at the window with his camera up to his eye, focusing on the three glamour girls across the square.

'She's *not* my hot new date,' Rob grunted, but he went and took a good look anyway.

'God, this wind is ruining my hair!' Marina complained, turning from Sinead to Frankie. 'Haven't *you* got a key with you?'

'No. Have you?'

'No pockets,' Marina pointed out. She'd dressed down in denim cut-offs and a boat-necked T-shirt for the drawing class, but pockets had spoiled the line of the trousers, so she'd sewn them all up. The wind blew stray blonde curls across her cheeks now, and her arms were covered in goosepimples. 'I wish I was like you,' she sighed to Frankie, as Sinead tipped the entire contents of her bag onto the doorstep.

'Meaning?' Frankie frowned. She guessed she wasn't going to like the answer.

'Well, you're so casual, you don't care what you look like,' Marina pointed out. 'I'm more high maintenance, if you know what I mean.'

I was right. I don't like it, Frankie thought. 'Yeah, I know what you mean,' she muttered.

Marina winced. *Me and my big mouth!* Thank heavens Sinead had found the stupid key at last.

'They're going inside!' Travis ran the commentary for Rob. 'Your one with the blonde hair is tottering in first. The wacky one in thigh-length boots is picking up her stuff. The leggy brunette's bending down to help her. Now they're all in the house, they're closing the door . . . They think it's all over . . . it is now!'

'Huh. What's on Sky?' Rob wondered, turning back to Teletext.

'Home sweet home!' Sinead sighed, running her hand through her short, fluffy hair. It had been light-blonde for a month. Tomorrow she planned to run a bright-red rinse through it, to match the retro corduroy jacket she'd picked up in the market. For now, though, there were boxes and black bin-bags in the hallway to clear, suitcases on the stairs to unpack. Wires from Frankie's sound system snaked across the living room, into the front lounge.

'When will your mum come back to check the place out?' Marina asked Sinead, lugging her giant case up two more steps before she grew exhausted and gave in.

'Not for ages. She went back to Dublin.'

'Who wants coffee?' Frankie asked, tackling the obstacle course into the kitchen. 'Bleeding Ikea!' she yelped, as she stumbled over a flat-pack chest of drawers.

Typical Mum! Sinead thought. *She buys a student house so I have somewhere to live. Cool. Then she fills it with stuff that needs assembling and sods off back to her man in Ireland!*

'Coffee!' Frankie announced. 'No milk. We ran out.' She put three mugs down in the middle of the living-room mess.

'We need a man!' Sinead sighed. She was fine with fabrics and scissors, pins and sewing machines, but furniture was not her thing. 'Men can actually turn stuff in these boxes into three-D objects you can sit on and eat off.'

There was a silence, then Marina said slowly, '*I* can find us a man . . .'

11

'Where? In Yellow Pages?' Sinead asked, wearily.

'No. The guy I met earlier.' Taking out her phone, Marina wandered through into the empty front room overlooking the square. It had beige walls, an old-fashioned radiator, tall, built-in bookshelves, and a long bay window down to the floor. She looked out of the window and across the square.

'Rob Leather-Jacket?' Sinead laughed. 'Am I wrong, or did you have one teensy-weensy, two-minute conversation while you had him pinned against the counter?'

'So? He's on my speed-dial.'

'Hang on!' Sinead protested. 'You can't invite him over. What if he turns out to be a weirdo?'

'He won't be, and I can.' *Beep-beep, bip.* She dialled the number.

'Stop her!' Sinead appealed to Frankie.

But Frankie was with Marina on this. 'The guy's a lab technician. He's probably ace with an Allen key!'

'Yep . . .?' said the laid-back, unsuspecting voice on the end of the phone.

'Hi, Rob!' Marina said in honey-sweet tones. 'This is Marina from Number 13 – we just met, remember?'

TWO

September 28th, 8.30pm
Hey, everyone out there. OK, so how come I'm not out partying? I know, it sucks. But a girl has to wash her hair and paint her nails once in a while.

Marina typed with two fingers, a towel wrapped around her wet hair, her computer resting on the little Ikea desk that Rob had laboriously assembled.

Today I found a Sixties miniskirt in Oxfam. Black-and-white zigzag fabric. Mary Quant-ish, very retro. Also found a man!!! Though he doesn't know it yet. Named Rob . . .

'Marina's blogging again!' Frankie sighed. She went and peered over Marina's shoulder. 'Watch out, Rob!'

'Who reads that stuff?' Sinead asked. She was busy unpacking essentials like hair-straighteners and fake tan.

'All Marina's fans out there in the ether!' Frankie explained. 'Hey, has anyone seen my phone?'

'Nope.'

'Nope.'

'Sinead, can you call me, so I can find it?' Frankie waited impatiently for the ringtone, then burrowed into a pile of cushions and came out triumphant.

Also got down and dirty today with a man I'd never met before, Marina typed.

'You wish!' Frankie laughed, reading again.

You could say he was an older type. Good body, though not sure if there was a brain up there.

'Yeah, yeah, yeah!' Frankie shoved Marina off her stool and typed a sentence: **She's talking about the male model in our life-drawing class – Frankie.**

'Thanks, pal!' Marina resumed her seat and logged off.

'What? I'm protecting your reputation. You

15

don't want the world thinking that you sleep with pervy old men!'

'Maybe she does,' Sinead said, savvily.

'Maybe I do,' Marina agreed.

'Yuck! Anyhow, I thought you were after Rob Leather-Jacket. Mr Muscles!' Frankie flopped down on the futon that Marina's man had recently assembled.

'Yeah, poor guy!' Sinead had kept Rob supplied with cups of coffee all the time he'd been busy with the Allen key. He'd arrived at 2.00pm and only just gone. One futon, two desks, a table and four chairs later, he'd left exhausted.

'You didn't hear him complaining, did you?' Marina asked, switching off her computer. All afternoon she'd smooched and smiled, pouted and batted her eyelashes at Rob. What on earth could he have to complain about?

'How was the hot date?' Travis asked, as Rob finally crawled back into their flat.

'Man, give me a beer!' Rob sighed. 'I never want to see another flat-pack as long as I live!'

*

'Whoah!' Frankie squealed, as the futon collapsed under her. She tipped onto the floor and rolled against a heap of cushions. 'The leg just gave way. Who put this thing up?'

Sinead pulled her to her feet. 'Rob did. Hey, did you hear what he said about his house-mate? Y'know – the cute one.'

'Yeah, he's a film and photography student at our place.' Marina's memory was razor-sharp where guys were concerned. 'Second year. Into music. Name of Travis. Why?'

'No reason,' Sinead muttered.

'Yeah, right, no reason!' Marina and Frankie laughed.

'As if butter wouldn't melt in your mouth!' Marina teased Sinead. 'Listen, if you fancy Travis, why not just admit it?'

Sinead frowned and backed off into the kitchen. 'How can I fancy him? I only saw him once, and that was from a distance.'

'It's enough,' Marina insisted, nudging Frankie. 'She does, she has a thing for Travis!'

'Let's all get dressed up!' Frankie said suddenly. 'C'mon, you've got fifteen minutes!'

'What for?' Sinead and Marina wanted to

know. 'What's the deal? Where are we going?'

'Party.'

'Party?' Marina's blue-grey eyes lit up. She *loved* parties. She was already deciding what to wear.

'Where?' Sinead asked.

'Here on the square, Number 26.' Frankie was already halfway up the stairs. 'Rob mentioned it. I haven't got a clue whose house it is, but he said he and Travis are gonna be there!'

'*Da-dah!*' Marina burst into Sinead's room in a pink-and-yellow sundress and a strappy pair of shoes.

'Too summery,' Sinead told her, and Marina vanished out of the door.

Next came Frankie, twirling in Levis and a blue V-neck over a white-and-blue striped top.

'Not dressy enough,' Sinead decided. 'But I like the necklace. How about me?'

Frankie studied Sinead's fitted, cream brocade top and gathered pink chiffon skirt. She had dressed the whole thing up with three-inch lilac heels. 'Knockout. No contest!' Frankie acknowledged. 'Where did you get the top?'

'Made it myself. And the skirt. Does it really look OK?'

'Uh-huh,' Frankie reassured her, then dashed off to change.

'Party-party-party!' Marina chanted, standing outside Number 26 dressed in a black strappy top and matching floaty skirt, with a pink ribbon tied around her waist. 'Happy birthday to you!' she sang, as the door was opened by a guy with streaked blond hair and wearing a black shirt.

'It's not my birthday,' he grinned, letting the three girls in anyway.

'This is my demure look,' Marina explained quietly, as she, Frankie and Sinead squeezed through the noisy crowd. 'I wanted to be subtle.'

'Why?' Frankie's eyebrows shot up.

'Don't want to frighten the horses,' came the enigmatic reply. Then Marina spotted Rob's leather jacket beside the sound system. She made a bee-line for him.

'Marina is *so* not subtle,' Sinead grinned, looking around for Travis.

'Yeah, I think she might be frightening the horses right about now,' Frankie agreed, as Marina backed Rob up against a speaker. 'She'd better watch they don't bolt.'

'It looks like he's the DJ.' Only half paying attention, Sinead scanned the room. She was searching for Travis's drop-dead gorgeous face, topped by spiky, brown hair. When she saw him, standing in a corner with a can, she drew in a sharp breath. Yup, she definitely fancied him, she decided.

'There's your guy!' Frankie followed Sinead's gaze. 'He's not with anyone. Go, girl! What are you waiting for?'

Sinead blushed, then grinned. 'Me? I'm deep-down subtle! Truly!'

'You mean shy?' Frankie couldn't believe it. Sinead was a babe. She had the looks and the style to pull any guy she wanted. Whereas she, Frankie, was more of an acquired taste. Guys at school had never swarmed around her, like they must have done with Marina and Sinead.

Frankie had ended up wearing the necklace Sinead had admired. She'd designed and made it herself – a high choker of tiny, transparent beads and dangling strands of silver wire. She'd teamed it with a black halter-neck top and jeans. Just one fashion statement – that was enough for her. She was never over the top. In fact, she was the kind of girl most blokes didn't even notice.

Whereas Sinead drew them like a honey pot. Here they were, already humming around her, offering to get her a drink, asking her name. Frankie sighed and scanned the room. Rob had escaped from Marina for a moment to change the track and was turning up the volume. The party was about to get going, big time.

'More drink!' Rob yelled at Travis. He mimed swallowing the contents of a can, indicating that he couldn't escape from his mixing deck.

'Here!' said Marina smoothly, handing him a lager. She'd thought ahead.

'Thanks,' he grunted.

'Dance?' she asked, taking him by the arm.

'Can't. I'm busy. Choose the next track if you like.'

'Wow, cool.' Marina put a finger thoughtfully to her luscious bottom lip. 'Hmm. Which one?

21

How about this?' She held the record so close that Rob had to lean in towards her. She admired his bare forearms as he took it from her. 'Do you work out?' she asked.

'Look at that!' Frankie laughed. 'Five seconds in and Marina's already up close and personal!'

'It's a rare talent,' Sinead agreed.

'Pity it's wasted on Rob, though.'

Mr Leather-Jacket was busy DJ-ing and ignoring Marina's signals.

'Maybe he's playing hard to get.' Sinead couldn't believe that Rob hadn't noticed Marina's super-charged tactics.

'Maybe,' Frankie conceded. 'Or maybe he just doesn't get it.'

'I tried everything!' Marina wailed, as she, Sinead and Frankie queued for the bathroom. They were standing halfway up the stairs, pressed against the wall as other party guests trailed up and down. Below them, the music thudded from Rob's mixing desk.

'We know. We saw,' Sinead said. 'Maybe he's immune to girls.'

Marina recoiled dramatically. 'You mean he's gay?'

'No way!' Frankie shook her head.

'No,' Sinead soothed. 'I mean, he just doesn't pick up the signals. Some guys don't.'

Frankie nodded. 'Yeah. A guy like Rob would rather be alone in front of the TV. If you made a move, all he'd be able to talk about was which idiot scored an own goal against Lichtenstein in the qualifying rounds of the European Cup.'

Marina considered this, then shook her head. 'I don't believe it. It's not possible.'

'Believe me,' Frankie told her. 'It happens.'

''Xcuse,' Travis muttered to Sinead, as he passed by. He caught her eye.

She noted his brown eyes and straight, dark eyebrows, his curvy mouth and full bottom lip . . .

'Travis!' Marina cried, grabbing his arm and following him downstairs. 'What's the story with your friend Rob? Has he said anything about me? Does he have a girlfriend? C'mon, tell me – I need to know!'

THREE

'In fashion you have to move fast,' Tristan Fox explained to the class. 'You need energy, creativity, the ability to communicate. You need brilliance!'

'Ugh!' Frankie pulled a face at Marina and Sinead. 'I drank way too much wine last night.'

'During your first year I will be teaching you how to design beautiful clothes and accessories. You will innovate. You will invent. You will be versatile!'

'Ouch!' Frankie groaned, clutching her head. She wasn't sure she was up to this.

Tristan perched on a high stool, one hand resting lightly on his knee. He was Mr Style, with his choppy haircut and fitted, blue, satin shirt. His voice was mid-Atlantic cool, his age indeterminate. 'I want you all to open your fashion folios and choose the piece of work from your entry collection that you're most proud of,' he told his students. 'Then be prepared to explain to the rest of us the design process that brought you to this piece.'

Marina bit her bottom lip. Tough call – there were half a dozen designs she could choose.

'Help!' Frankie muttered under her breath. She opened her portfolio. Where was that chunky necklace design? It was the only halfway-decent thing she could think of.

Sinead considered her Chloe-inspired jacket – the one with slashes cut into the sleeves and a heavy chain linking the top and lower pockets.

'You're three years out of date,' Tristan told her, passing by. Then he picked up Frankie's design for the silver necklace. 'What gave you the idea for this?' he asked.

Frankie's voice shook as she answered. 'I looked at some graffiti on the Underground and came up with this curved cross.'

'Bold and interesting. However, also rather passé. How about this?' Tristan had moved on to Marina's work. He pointed to a design for a beaded mini-dress, draped with suede fringe and gold lace. 'Where did this come from?'

'I was inspired by the movies from the Thirties.' Marina's confidence set her apart. 'I wanted a high halter-neck and a straight line, then I added contemporary touches, like the suede.'

Their teacher studied the drawings closely. 'Too Versace-derivative,' he decided.

'Is that a bad thing?' Marina asked, totally up-front.

A tiny frown appeared on Tristan's Botoxed brow, then it cleared. 'Not necessarily,' he admitted, moving swiftly on.

'Marina, how could you challenge Tristan Fox? I nearly died!' Frankie exclaimed later. The girls had regrouped for coffee after their first class of the day. 'I mean, *Tristan Fox*!'

'He works for Charles Jourdan!' Sinead pointed out. 'He's only the number one guy in town for shoes!'

'I didn't like the way he dissed our work,' Marina shrugged. 'We're only first years, for God's sake.'

'I'll be glad when the practical workshops start,' Sinead agreed. 'Give me a pair of scissors and I'm happy.'

'Yeah, and then we get to visit the shows and the trade fairs,' Frankie reminded them.

'Paris!' Sinead sighed.

'Milan. New York!' Marina dreamed of the glittering international catwalks.

'Tucson!' Frankie grinned.

'Tucson?' Marina and Sinead came down to earth with a bump.

'Yeah – Tucson, Arizona. It hosts the biggest semi-precious gem fair in the world. Tourmalines as big as your thumbnail!'

'Wow!' the others said, flatly.

Frankie tutted, then picked up her bag.

'Cool bag,' Sinead said, admiring the denim rucksack with red embroidered patches sewn onto it. 'Did you make it?'

'Yep. Now, I don't know about you guys, but I have to go to my first jewellery class. See you later!'

'Wait for me!' Marina left her half-empty coffee cup and darted after Frankie. 'You can show me where the jewellery workshop is.'

Frankie strode ahead, along the corridor, down a flight of steps. 'I can? Why?'

'Let's just say I have a little technical problem with my first project.'

Frankie frowned. 'But you haven't started your project yet . . . Oh, I get it!'

'. . . A technical problem that maybe a certain jewellery lab technician can help me solve.'

'Marina!' Frankie warned, pushing open the wrong door and quickly retreating.

'What?'

'This Rob guy – you're coming on too strong.'

Marina fluffed up her hair and smoothed down her crop-top. '*Moi?*'

Finding the right door, Frankie stood in the entrance to the workshop. 'Yes, you!' she warned.

'You're late,' the teacher snapped at the newcomers. 'Find a seat.'

'B-but—!' Marina began to explain.

'I said, sit!'

Marina sat.

'Which is how, by mistake I attended my first and last lecture on the history of European jewellery,' Marina told Sinead as they all walked home from college. She did a Marilyn Monroe wiggle on the pavement and sang a line from 'Diamonds Are A Girl's Best Friend'.

'*These rocks won't lose their shape!*' Sinead joined in.

'*Diamonds are a girl's best friend!*' they all chorused, as the sea of office-workers ahead of them parted.

'What did you think of Claudia Brown?' Frankie asked Marina.

'Scary lady!' came the answer, as Marina crossed her forefingers to fend off the vampire. The lecturer was only five-foot two, with long, jet-black hair scraped back from a sharp, pointed face. But her voice had packed the punch of an army sergeant major.

'She designs jewellery for most of the big families in Europe,' Frankie told them. 'Did a Danish royal wedding. Or Dutch. Which was it?'

'So you didn't get to see Mr Muscles?' Sinead asked Marina. 'Don't come over all innocent – I know that's why you went with Frankie in the first place!'

'So?'

'I *told* her she was coming on too strong,' Frankie said. 'I mean, last night at the party, even Travis warned you not to get too far in Rob's face. He said you'd scare him off. And guess what – you did.'

'Yeah, and I notice shy little Miss Sinead and Travis ended up together – *not*!'

'Thanks for reminding me!' Sinead muttered.

'No, I'm just saying, if that's where being subtle gets you – by yourself in a corner, watching every other girl in the place chat your guy up – well, no thanks!'

'Hey, you two.' Frankie came in between Sinead and Marina. 'So it wasn't the best party for pulling guys.' She shrugged. In fact, all three of them had left alone, crossing the square together at two in the morning, while Travis had stayed behind to help Rob pack up his decks.

'The humiliation!' Marina whimpered, pulling up her collar to assume a disguise.

It was rush hour and Walgrave Square was jammed with noisy traffic. 'Anyway, I'm thinking that maybe Travis isn't boyfriend material,' Sinead said, raising her voice above the horns. 'We could be mates, though.'

Frankie and Marina stared.

Sinead dug herself a deeper hole. 'He's too much of a bimbo, there's probably nothing going on inside his head.'

More silence, backed by the roar of traffic.

'Listen, I'm not going to compete for his attention with a dozen other women.'

'I can't believe I'm hearing this!' Marina gasped.

Sinead couldn't explain. She'd been a spectator on this kind of stuff when she was a kid. Great-looking guy – babe-magnet – gets flirted with at parties while his partner looks on; guy is eventually tempted – cheats on his wife; wife finds out – end of marriage. That was the story of her mum and dad, and she didn't want the same thing happening to her.

But maybe she should lighten up. After all, Travis *was* her ideal guy – shy and sensitive, with those gorgeous, dark-brown eyes.

'Yeah, we'll be mates,' she told Marina and Frankie decisively, as they passed the front steps of Number 45.

'Hey!' Travis flung open a lower window and hung out over the street.

'What happened to you?' Frankie asked, taking in his drenched T-shirt and panicked face.

'Washing machine,' he yelled. 'Gone ballistic – foam everywhere. How the hell do you turn it off?'

'How sad is that?' Marina laughed. She'd kicked off her shoes and waded across the kitchen, turned a few knobs, and now the machine sat quietly in the corner. 'All you have to do is this, this and this!'

'You probably put too much powder in,' Frankie told Travis, gazing at the scummy foam under the table.

'The thing was coming at me! It was juddering and moving across the tiles, I swear!' A shocked Travis had to sit down to recover.

'The Night of the Undead!' Frankie joined in with Marina's wave of giggles. 'Washing machine wakes from uneasy slumber – threatens to take over the world!'

'I've never used one before,' he explained, sheepishly.

'Obviously.' This was the first time Sinead had spoken to Travis, and it had come out sarcastic, not at all what she'd intended.

'How long have you lived here?' Marina demanded, perching on the table and letting the suds drip from her bare toes.

'A year. It's Rob's place. He rents me a room.'

'How about the dishwasher – can you work that?'

'Nope.'

'The microwave?' Marina demanded.

'Yeah, I guess.' Travis was beginning to recover. He blushed and grinned. 'Hey, thanks for rescuing me,' he told them.

'Lucky we were passing.' Frankie grinned back. 'And listen, I'll let you into a secret – I don't know how to work a washing machine either. I'm a total technophobe.'

'Me too – like, do you understand the principles of the internal combustion engine?' Travis quizzed.

'Nope. How about the microchip?'

'Nope. I can work out the mechanism of the zoom lens though.'

'Yeah, I heard you were into photography. Do you ever take stuff like jewellery for magazine shoots – that kind of thing?'

Soon Frankie and Travis were deep in conversation.

'Yuck, how am I going to get down from here?' Marina wailed, noticing for the first time that there were soggy pizza crusts and bits of cardboard floating in the soapy puddles under the table.

'Wait, I'll find something to clean it up with,' Sinead promised. Mrs Mop. How cool was that? She opened a cupboard under the sink, then stepped aside as a heap of soccer boots and muddy trainers plopped out.

'Come and take a look at my Nikon,' Travis invited Frankie, leading her into the living room.

Marina swung her legs like a toddler. 'Help!'

'How?' Sinead cried, staring down at her own ruined shoes. The dead washing machine winked at her with its evil, red eye.

'Frankie seems to have hit it off with Travis!' Marina hissed.

'Yeah, fantastic.' Sinead scowled. There she was, wading through scum, about to burst into tears. 'Where's the freaking mop?'

'In the yard,' Rob said, coming in through the back door. He put his bike helmet down on the work surface, then glanced across at Marina. 'OK,' he said, ready to blame the first person he could lay his hands on. 'So what happened?'

FOUR

'Time to back off,' Marina decided. A full week after the curious incident of the washing machine, even she could see that her full-on tactics with Rob weren't producing the desired result.

'For ever?' Sinead asked. It was Friday evening and Marina had just signed off from her on-line diary.

'Don't be silly.'

'For how long then?'

'As long as it takes.' *No signal*, her computer told her with a whine and a click.

Can you believe it — I fancy the only guy in the whole world who doesn't fancy me back! she'd blogged. **Not that I'm big-headed!**

. . . Watch this space! Frankie had added.

'Yeah, well, I'm backing off from Travis too,' Sinead said. There was more to life than lusting after the unattainable, like trawling through the fabric stalls in the local market, for instance, and finding the most exquisite, end-of-roll length of beaded, black satin.

'So what's new?' Marina teased. 'Like you've been paying him loads of attention – *not!*'

'He has to make the first move,' Sinead explained. Since the suds episode, she'd seen Travis a couple of times – once going into his house, once when he came to see Frankie about a camera Frankie was considering buying. Both times she'd blanked him.

'I can't believe you're a twenty-first-century girl!' Marina wailed. 'Y'know, it's the new millennium. A woman is allowed to make a move on a man!'

'Marina's right,' Frankie said, thoughtfully.

'I am? Wow!' Marina checked her hair.

'Just this once, yeah.' Frankie was at the bathroom mirror, fixing her mascara and calling out down the stairs. 'Sinead, it's pretty clear that Travis doesn't even know you're interested.'

Sinead sat cross-legged on the futon, tugging at a tassel on one of the cushions. 'Maybe. Anyway, he likes you, Frankie.'

A clatter on the bare stairs told Marina and Sinead that Frankie was on her way down. 'Yeah, he likes talking to me about thirty-six exposure black-and-white films,' she pointed out, doing her usual putting-herself-down thing. 'Focus distances and exposure times, developers and enlargers, digital versus film.' No way was there anything between them.

'Does he ever mention me?' Sinead wanted to know.

Frankie shook her head. 'Why? Do you want me to say something to him?'

'No!' Sinead shot up from the futon. 'Don't! If you ever do that, I'll kill you!'

'She means yes,' Marina said.

'No! Don't, Frankie! I couldn't bear it.'

'She means no,' Frankie reported back to Marina, who shrugged and reglossed her already-slicked lips.

'Let's go!' Marina said, popping her lippy into her bag. It was a pity that Rob didn't know what he was missing, but no way was she going to let it get in the way of her having a good time tonight.

'Where to?' Frankie asked.

Sinead slipped her feet into her highest shoes – a pair of primrose yellow Guccis – an eighteenth-birthday present from her mum.

They were through the front door. The street lights were glowing pinky-orange, the pavements dampened by a misty rain.

'To this great bar in the city centre,' Miranda told them. 'It's supposed to be the trendiest place in town!'

Fashion students were meant to be super-cool. They were long-legged and beautiful and earned money modelling on the side. They killed guys dead with one smoking, sultry glance. That was the story anyhow.

Only, it didn't quite work that way for Frankie and Sinead.

Take Frankie. She'd been at Central for two weeks now, trying to slot into place. She had the legs and the looks, but her confidence was zero.

'You're kidding!' Sinead had said on the first

Thursday of term. She and Frankie had been having a night in, trying out cleansers and toners on their jaded skins. 'What d'you mean, you hate walking into a crowded room by yourself?'

'It's true,' Frankie had sighed. 'I've been this way since I was a little kid. Sometimes I get to the workshop and I have to psych myself up just to push the door open. Deep breaths, count to ten . . . and sometimes I just turn around and walk away.'

'So how come you're always smiling?' Sinead asked, lying back on her bed with Gentle Rose Exfoliator plastered onto her neck and elbows.

'Am I?' Frankie took up a Pilates position on the floor by the window. 'Smiling is my thing. It gets me through.'

'Not waving, but drowning,' Sinead murmured.

'What?'

'Not waving, but drowning. It's from a poem. This woman is too far out at sea, trying to get attention. Everyone on the shore thinks she's being friendly, but she's not waving, she's drowning.'

'Right!' Frankie agreed. 'Not laughing but

choking. That's what it feels like.' It was cool discussing this stuff with Sinead and feeling that she understood.

And then Sinead had closed her eyes and told Frankie about her mother. How much money she had, and how her mum liked to be called Daniella so that strangers would mistake them for sisters. 'She buys Max Mara and Hugo Boss. *Harpers & Queen* is her bible.'

'Is that bad?' Frankie wanted to know.

Sinead sighed. 'She lets me do my own thing, I guess.'

'But you wish she baked apple pies?'

'Something like that. Hey, listen to me! Let's change the subject. What about Marina? Now she's definitely the girl who has it all!'

'Don't you believe it,' Frankie said, shaking her head. 'OK, so she looks like a girl with "For Display Purposes Only" stuck all over her. But there's more going on there.'

'But what? What *is* going on there?'

There was no reply as Frankie took a deep breath and tried to rebalance her inner core. 'I don't know,' she said at last. 'Let's wait and see, hey?'

'*Gonna wash that man right outta my hair!*' Marina sang, Hollywood-style. '*And send him on his way!*'

'God, where do you drag those ancient songs up from?' Frankie groaned. The three of them were glammed up and on their way to the trendy bar.

'Mitzy Gaynor in *South Pacific*, nineteen-fifties. The boned swimsuit, the short, bubbly perm, the Cleopatra eyebrows . . .'

'We get the picture,' Sinead cut in.

They approached the queue to get into the bar, took one look and turned around.

'I don't do queues,' Marina announced.

'Hey, Frankie!' Travis called from across the street. He and Rob were heading into The Alex. 'Fancy a beer?'

'Why not?' Frankie agreed, dodging the cars. 'Come on, you two.'

Marina and Sinead hung back.

'Come *on*!' Frankie insisted.

'Not part of the plan,' Marina muttered. On the other hand, she knew she looked her best, after a two-hour session of straighteners, gels,

THE FASHION
RETAIL ACADEMY
LIBRARY

Renewals:
020 7307 2367
library@fashionretailacademy.ac.uk

15 GRESSE STREET LONDON

creams, brushes, pencils and perfumes. Even Rob had to notice. 'Here we go!' she told Sinead, sashaying across the street.

Sinead paused to take her phone out of her bag and answer it. 'Hi, Mum. Yeah, fine. Cool. OK, see you.' By the time she hung up, she had no choice but to follow the others into the student bar.

Inside The Alex, it was sweaty, noisy and crowded. Sinead had to push through a barrier of blokes before she could pick out Marina's blonde head and Frankie's lit-up smile. Frankie was joking with Travis, who listened and nodded, said something in Frankie's ear that made her burst out laughing, then turned to take his drink from Rob.

'Hey, Sinead!' Marina spotted her and waved. 'What kept you?' she asked, after Sinead had pushed her way through the crowd.

'Daniella was on the phone. She's back in England.'

'Your mother? Oh my God, does that mean she'll be checking up on the house?' Marina gasped. 'We need to unpack, make it tidy, do some – er – cleaning!'

'Don't panic.' Sinead grinned as she pictured Marina in a pair of Marigolds. 'If the place is a wreck, Mum will pay for a cleaner.'

'She will?'

'Yeah.'

'Cool.' Marina relaxed. She took a drink from Rob. 'Sinead drinks Bacardi Breezers,' she told him, sweetly.

He turned back to the bar.

'How's it going with Leather-Jacket?' Sinead whispered.

Marina raised her eyebrows. 'This baby is one *big* challenge! Listen, I need a topic of conversation.'

'Try football,' Sinead suggested, laughing at Marina's panicked expression. 'OK, motor-bikes?' she went on.

'Motorbikes . . .' Marina echoed, then shook her head. Then: 'So tell me, Rob, what's your favourite movie? Who's your favourite actress?'

Rob shrugged, and handed Sinead her drink. 'What is this, a job interview?'

'Kind of.' Marina smiled enigmatically. 'What star sign are you? Let me guess – you're a Scorpio!'

Still laughing, Sinead edged away to give Marina more space, backing into Travis and making him spill his drink over Frankie.

'This Fuji I had – it was OK, but the definition wasn't great,' Travis was telling Frankie.

'Whoah!' Frankie yelped as the beer trickled down her chest. 'Don't even *think* about it!' she warned Travis, as he reached out to wipe her down.

He grinned, then watched Frankie and Sinead head off to the Ladies. Before they were even halfway across the room, two girls he'd never seen before had hit on him and dragged him away.

'Yeah, Scorpio!' Marina declared. 'That means you're sociable and fun to be with, but sometimes you can be too laid-back.'

'Sounds like me,' Rob agreed. He frowned to find himself left alone at the bar with Marina Bombshell. Women like her scared him to death.

Marina had never pushed a heavy rock up a hill, but if she had, she knew this was what it would feel like. 'How long have you worked at Central?'

'Couple of years.'

'Do you like your job?'

'It's a job.'

'What's your favourite thing then? Is it riding your bike out in the countryside?' Wow, she was getting desperate. *Come back, Sinead. Come back, Frankie!* 'Hey, listen,' she said, swerving suddenly away from the dead-end of Harley Davidsons and Kawasakis. Maybe the smoke, the hullaballoo and the heat had gone to her head. 'Did you know that my mate, Sinead, fancies your best mate?'

'Huh?' Rob had hardly heard a single word she'd said. 'You talking about Travis?'

Marina nodded. This had better be quick. She could see Sinead and Frankie making their way back to the bar, and Sinead would definitely kill her if she found out what she was doing. 'They're not getting it together because both parties are too scared to make a move. Whoops!' A shove in the back from a stranger sent Marina tottering against Rob.

Trying to ignore her cleavage, Rob took a long drink and swallowed hard. 'I hear you,' he muttered, though the entire conversation had been drowned by the racket going on around them.

'So, anyway, I've got this plan. We're gonna have a party at our place tomorrow, and *you* have to tell *Travis* what I've just told you – y'know, set him up in advance. Only don't let anyone know you've said anything. Get it?'

Rob breathed in Marina's Dolce & Gabbana perfume. It rocked his senses, along with the plunging neckline and the baby-woman voice. 'Got it.'

'Good.' Marina was pleased with herself. She'd done Sinead one great big favour, and she felt that sharing this little secret with Rob might be a way for her and him to get closer.

'Where did Travis go?' Frankie asked, when she and Sinead finally made it through the crush.

Marina broke away from Rob with one last, lingering look. 'You promise to tell Travis?' she said, quietly.

'Yeah, I'll do it. I'll tell him right now.' Taking his drink with him, Rob melted into the bloke-barrier by the door.

'Promise to tell Travis *what*?' Frankie asked suspiciously, as Sinead joined them.

Marina's eyes sparkled. 'That we're having a party – tomorrow.'

'We are?' This was news to Sinead, and it didn't exactly fit in with the possibility that Daniella might drop by. But then, she never said no to a party. 'Cool,' she agreed. 'Let's invite everyone from the course.'

'Hey, mate,' Rob said, as he finally managed to drag the two rampant strangers off Travis. 'I've been told to tell you something.'

'Go ahead.' Travis appreciated the break. One full-on girl he could handle, but two were too much.

'It turns out that the blonde isn't after me.'

'No hot date?' Travis asked, casting a casual glance towards Sinead, Marina and Frankie. 'We're talking about Marina, right?'

'Yeah, that one. What d'you know?' Rob laughed, passing on Marina's none too subtle, half-audible message. 'You've been reading the signals all wrong, mate.'

'How come?' Travis caught Marina's eye and

somehow found he couldn't do his usual thing of looking quickly down. Instead, he gave her a cheesy stare.

'It's you Marina fancies, Trav. She just told me, straight out.'

'Me?' Travis let his jaw drop.

'Yeah, they're having a party at their place. Tomorrow night. And don't say I didn't warn you.'

FIVE

'Let's talk technical!' Frankie enthused. 'I want to know how many pixels per square centimetre you need to get good enough definition to take pictures of my jewellery projects.'

Travis nodded. 'You're talking professional quality. That kind of digital camera costs three times as much as a single lens reflex, but the advantage with a digital is that you can load it straight into your PC, choose the best image on-screen and print it off. With an SLR you have to wait for the film to be processed.'

'Yeah, I get that,' Frankie said. 'But I don't think my student loan will run to a decent digital.'

'Don't tell me, two weeks in and you're already overdrawn.'

'No, really!' Frankie insisted. 'I'm not like Sinead and Marina – I don't have the cash.'

Travis warmed more to Frankie every time they met. Her brain was connected directly to her mouth – no games involved. 'Not a spoilt little rich kid?'

Frankie glanced down at her frayed jeans and Topshop sweater. She shrugged, then laughed. 'Don't get me wrong – I'm not saying that Sinead and Marina are spoilt. Sinead's mother *is* loaded, though.'

'Sinead's the wacky one, right?' Rob broke in. He'd been stripping down the brakes from his bike and had oily parts lined up on newspaper spread out on the kitchen table.

'Yeah, and Marina looks like Marilyn Monroe,' Frankie reminded him.

Rob raised an eyebrow at Travis, who blanked him.

'Listen, Frankie, about this camera – why don't I lend you an old single lens reflex of mine for you to practise with? It's a Nikon, but not the latest model. You can take the pictures, then bring the film along to me. I'll develop it for you.'

Frankie took a step backwards, slam into the overflowing rubbish bin by the sink. 'You serious?'

'Yeah, why not? I'm a photography student, remember.'

'You'd do that for me?'

'Read my lips,' Travis told her. 'As long as you take care of it, you can borrow my camera, no problem. Wait here. I'll go get it.'

Clink-clunk went the metal bits on the table as Rob wiped and buffed. 'You must be flavour of the month,' he told Frankie. 'Normally wild horses couldn't come between Travis and his Nikon.'

Frankie pulled a face. It was weird to hear via Rob that Travis actually *liked* her. 'Oh God, now watch me go and lose it!' she muttered. By the time Travis came downstairs again, she was a bag of nerves. But, boy was she grateful.

'I'll run through the basics,' Travis offered. 'It's automatic focus, but you can override that by pushing this button here . . .'

'Where *were* you?' Marina demanded, when Frankie finally got back to the house. She and

Sinead had had to order the booze for the party and bring it back home by themselves.

'Across the square. Travis lent me a camera.'

'Sssh!' Marina warned. 'Don't let her hear you.'

'Why not? Where is she?' Seeing that preparations for the party had started, Frankie began taking cans out of a box and stacking them in the fridge.

'Gone to fetch the last load in from the cab. Listen, Frankie, you don't want Sinead to be jealous of you and Travis, do you?'

'No chance! Travis is strictly a mate.'

'Sinead doesn't know that. In any case, how can you be sure?' In Marina's experience, friendships across the genders were never that simple. Like, *never*. 'Listen, Frankie—'

'How come everyone's saying "Listen, Frankie" to me all of a sudden?'

'Listen! I don't want you spoiling my little plan.' Marina flinched as she bent back a fingernail on a sealed cardboard box containing bottles of red wine. The nail stayed in one piece, and she flapped her hand and breathed a sigh of relief.

'What little plan?' Frankie asked, rescuing cans that were rolling out of the fridge onto the floor.

'To get Travis and Sinead together,' Marina whispered.

Frankie stood up straight and looked Marina in the eye. 'You haven't told him she fancies him, have you? You promised, remember!'

'*No-oh!*'

'You *have* – you told Travis!'

'I did not. Anyway, *ssh*! She's bringing the stuff in now.'

The back door swung open and Sinead came in with half a bakery of fresh French bread.

'Yum!' Marina swooned. 'Don't you just love the smell of that stuff!'

'You *told* him!' Frankie hissed behind Sinead's back.

'Did not!' Marina hissed back. 'I'm not that stupid, OK!'

'Mate, it's gonna take me all bloody weekend to get the bike back in working order,' Rob complained. He and Travis were taking in the football round-up on Sky.

'Man U only drew with Portsmouth,' Travis noted.

'It needs new brake pads, plus I'm giving it a full service before its first MOT.'

'No sweat if you don't make it to this party tonight,' Travis acknowledged. 'I might give it a miss as well.'

'What, and turn down the chance of rampant sex with Marilyn – Miranda?' Rob shook his head in disbelief.

'Marina,' Travis reminded him. 'Hey, I'm sick of women throwing themselves at me!'

Flicking Travis's feet off the sofa, Rob sat down beside him. 'You serious?'

'Yeah . . . no!' Travis grinned. 'But Marina's not really my type.'

'So, what is your type?' Rob flicked channels. 'Hey, bloody Bolton beat Everton.'

'Me? I like understated women – not too much make-up, not too pushy, but still sexy.'

'You mean like, what's her name – Frankie?'

'No, not Frankie. She's just a good kid.'

'We're talking eighteen, aren't we? That's not a kid.'

'Yeah, but we're mates, Frankie and me. Look – Greenaway scored for Newcastle.'

'Mates!' Rob snorted in derision. Never in his two years at Central had he seen a babe-magnet like Travis and fashion-model material like Frankie stay just good friends. 'So I reckon I'll stay in tonight and finish the brakes,' he decided.

'Me too.' Travis didn't much fancy being cornered by man-hungry Marina.

'Did we buy enough booze?' Sinead panicked.

'This dress or these trousers with this top?' Frankie demanded.

'Who took my hair dryer?' Marina wailed.

The house was ready – strung with coloured paper lanterns, with speakers wired up in both downstairs rooms. Sinead had made gallons of fruit punch with a ton of sliced oranges, lemons and apples floating in it.

'Ice cubes!' Frankie remembered. 'I'll go and pick some up from the off-licence.'

'CDs!' Marina rummaged in the bottom of her suitcase for her latest albums.

C U 2moro! Sinead texted her mother.

Daniella had texted her to say she was going to drop by. *Worry about that later*, Sinead told herself.

'The thing is, I put women *way* down the list,' Rob tried to convince Travis, digging the grime out from behind his fingernails.

Travis lay stretched out on the sofa, watching *Match of the Day*.

'Women come after bikes, football, music, going down the gym, booze . . .'

'That's not normal,' Travis sighed. 'Talking to women can be cool.'

'Talking!' Rob laughed. 'Yeah, talking. Is that what you were doing with that girl behind the bar at The Alex last week?'

'She was putting it way out there. What was I meant to do? Anyhow, what about the one you pulled?'

'Slapper. Final score four-one, no contest,' Rob sighed, flicking off the match. 'Are you thirsty?'

'I could murder a pint,' Travis admitted. 'What time is it?'

'Ten forty-five. We'll just make it before last

orders. C'mon, Trav, move your bloody backside.'

'Travis and Rob aren't here!' Marina cornered Frankie in a thirty-second break from dancing in the front room. 'I don't understand what's happened.'

'They changed their minds,' Frankie shrugged. She didn't care – she was having a great time. The house was heaving, the music blasting out across the dark square.

'How could they *not* come? I mean, you were right – I *did* tell Rob to tell Travis about Sinead,' Marina confessed.

'Marina, you didn't!' Frankie yelled. But hey, why was she surprised?

'Yeah, and see what he's missing. Look at Sinead in that blue dress!' It was Jean Paul Gaultier: mousseline satin slashed and laced down the bodice like a Samurai warrior. 'Daniella's cast-off!' Marina sighed.

'It's cool, she's having fun,' Frankie decided. 'Who cares if Travis is here or not?'

Music spilled out into Walgrave Square as Rob

and Travis sprinted for the pub. The front door of Number 13 hung wide open, the house glowed and hummed.

'Free booze?' Rob said, pausing by a park bench.

Travis considered the pros and cons, nodded and changed course.

They made it to the party just before the fruit punch ran out.

SIX

For the first couple of hours of the party, the girls danced and the blokes watched. The house was bursting at the seams with students from Central.

Both blokes and girls consumed industrial quantities of alcohol.

'I'm pished!' Frankie giggled. 'Mar-ina-*ah*, are you as pished as me? Shan-ead, you're pished too!'

They were in a gaggle of girls on the dance floor, heads floating, brains disengaged.

'Not me. I'm totally in control,' Marina insisted, head thrown back, shuffling unsteadily from one bare foot to the other.

'Yeah, I'm smashed,' Sinead sighed happily. The ceiling was tilting at an interesting angle, unless she cocked her head to one side and made it go horizontal again.

'Great party,' Travis told them, as he crossed the floor in search of more beer.

Shock rooted the girls to the spot.

'He's here!' Marina squeaked, falling against Sinead.

Sinead gulped as her blurred gaze followed Travis's broad back and tousled head across the room. 'So?'

'So go, girl!' Marina ordered.

'Yeah, go get him, Sinead,' Frankie echoed. 'What the hell.'

But Sinead shook her head and slipped into a lilting Dublin accent. 'God, no! There's no way *I* do the chasing. Rule number one – make *them* make the first move.'

'What's rule number two?' Frankie asked. 'No tongues until you're engaged?'

'It's that stupid convent education,' Marina laughed, getting behind Sinead and trying to push her in Travis's direction. 'What do you expect of an all-girls school?'

'Quit it!' Sinead protested. 'Rob, help!' she cried, reaching out to the nearest person and grabbing him around the neck.

Rob staggered backwards, then caught Sinead around the waist. 'Hey, how come I lucked out?' he grinned.

Marina whirled round to face Rob. 'Did you tell him?' she demanded. Without waiting for an answer, she spun around again and blundered into a huddle of dancers as she staggered across the room after Travis.

'Dance?' Rob suggested to Sinead.

'Yeah – why not?' This was a good track, Rob was holding her upright so that the ceiling stayed in almost the right place, and dancing together seemed like a cool thing to do.

Travis made his pit-stop. He grabbed an extra beer for Rob, then got waylaid by a second-year girl from the Moving Images course. The two of them had been an item for about six weeks during their first year.

'Hey, Travis.'

'Hey, Suzy.' He got an eyeful of cleavage and a flick from a dangly earring as she leaned in to kiss him on the cheek.

'What're you up to these days?'

'Not a lot. You?'

'Just dumped my last boyfriend. How about you? Got anyone special?'

'Not right now.' *Wrong answer*. Travis kicked himself.

'Hmm.' Suzy gave him her killer look. 'I still think you're cute, you know.'

'Thanks, Suzy, but no thanks.' He'd given it a split-second's thought then decided, *Don't go there!* Suzy loved herself too much and got upset if she wasn't centre of attention, even for a nano-second.

A dazed frown appeared on her face. 'Screw you!' she muttered, before she moved on.

Bye, Suzy, nice to see you, too! Travis looked round and spotted Rob dancing with a girl in a blue dress. He caught the back view of the girl, took in the endless legs, the skinny waist, the bare arms wound around Rob's neck, then the couple turned and he recognised Sinead.

Huh! Now it was his turn to frown, though he didn't exactly know why, except that the back view had hit him between the eyes – the arms, the shoulders, and the long slits and glimpses of backbone through that shiny blue stuff.

Then when he saw the face resting against Rob's chest, eyes half-closed . . .

'Hey, Travis!' Marina moved in – red, red, *red*! There was practically no top to the scarlet dress – no straps, just a band across the boobs, a big keyhole cut into the bodice, showing a pierced belly-button, then the tightest skirt ever invented, like she'd been poured into it in liquid form. Red lips, half-open.

'Hey,' Travis muttered, shell-shocked. Had he told Rob that he liked his women understated and not too in your face? Man, what had he been thinking?

'I'm Marina,' she reminded him, catching the stunned look in his eyes but expecting it as her right.

'I know.' The grey-blue gaze, the black mascara, the bare shoulders, the red almost-dress . . . Travis offered Marina the beer that he'd brought for Rob.

'God, I'm smashed!' she laughed. 'I've got a message . . . something you need to know.' Marina realised that you couldn't trust guys like Rob to do these things, you had to do them yourself. Only now she was finding herself unexpectedly drawn to Travis herself. He had style, with his double layer of T-shirts, brown on top of white, and his big-buckled belt around slinky snake-hips.

Travis shrugged. 'You wanna dance?'

Marina pouted. Something had gone wrong here. She tried to work it out, then gave it up. 'Yep,' she nodded.

And Travis wrapped his arm around her shoulder and led her onto the dance floor.

Frankie danced until she dropped. She didn't care who she danced with, or for how long. She even danced by herself, there in the middle of the floor, when no one else was left standing.

'Great party,' people said, as they drifted away or found an empty corner of the house to kip in.

'Wimps,' she told them, dancing on.

She only stopped when the music did, which was when a neighbour called the police.

'Time to go home,' the policewoman told Frankie nicely.

'This *is* home!' Frankie cried. 'Where's

everyone gone? What time is it?'

'It's three-thirty in the morning, love. The woman next door wants to get some sleep.'

Fair enough. End of party. Frankie went to the kitchen and drank gallons of water, looked down at the rolling, empty beer cans on the floor, then scooped a couple of orange segments out of the drained punch bowl. The fruit tasted of vodka and cranberry juice. Yum.

But she was wrecked, it was time to get to bed.

Better lock up. Just check the back garden first, to make sure she wasn't locking anyone out.

'Dark,' she mumbled, tripping over the step. 'Yep, good job I checked.' There was a couple out here, snogging away in the moonlight. A girl in a red dress, a guy in a dark T-shirt, too into their own thing to notice Frankie.

Frankie scuffed her feet and gave a little cough.

The girl broke away from the clinch.

'Marina!' Frankie gasped and stepped back.

Travis looked round.

'Travis!' Stunned, Frankie stumbled back into the kitchen and went looking for Sinead to give her the bad news. Marina was well out of order. You should never do stuff like that to a friend!

Frankie ran upstairs, her heart thumping. She tried Sinead's room, but it was empty. Downstairs again, stumbling over lost shoes and discarded jackets, she looked in the front room, then out into the hallway. Try the front garden . . .

Jeez, another couple locked in each other's arms! What was happening? The world's longest snog-fest? Frankie shook her head in dismay.

Ouch. She shouldn't have done that. She'd lost another few million brain cells there. Hey, that leather jacket was familiar . . . It was the one that was normally grafted to Rob's back like a second skin. 'Rob?' Frankie asked hesitantly. 'Have you seen Sinead?'

Which was when Sinead finally broke away from Rob, swayed and caught hold of the front gate for support.

Travis and Marina. Rob and Sinead. *Wow!*

And now Marina was in the kitchen blubbing her eyes out, Travis was striding down the hallway, collaring Rob and heading off across the square before Frankie could say anything. Sinead collapsed into Frankie's arms.

'This was so *not* meant to happen!' Frankie wailed. Travis and Marina, Rob and Sinead. 'Like, has the world gone crazy, or what?'

SEVEN

Sunday – sore heads and mega regrets! Marina
blogged.

Frankie read over her shoulder, tutted,
then went upstairs to knock on Sinead's
door.

'Go away!' Sinead groaned.

Sighing, Frankie went and sat in the front
room amongst the debris of the party.

What's a girl supposed to do? Marina typed.
**A hunk like Travis comes on strong, and I'm
meant to turn him down? No way!** But she
wasn't happy writing this, so she logged off and
went to find Frankie.

'It wasn't my fault,' she began. 'Anyhow,
Sinead went off with Rob first, and she knows I
fancy him!'

'Yeah, yeah.' Frankie stared out of the window at the autumn leaves on the trees, her fingers curled round a scalding mug of black coffee. 'I don't like the way you use that computer as your conscience.'

'But it wasn't my *fault*. I mean, I did my best to get Sinead together with Travis. And what does she do? She only gets off with Rob instead!'

'I don't think she's talking to us any more,' Frankie warned.

Clutching her towelling dressing-gown tightly around her chest, Marina flopped down onto a floor-cushion. 'I did *try* to say sorry. You saw me.'

'I don't remember,' Frankie sighed. All she could recall was Marina blubbing, a bit of a scuffle on the stairs as Marina tried to stop Sinead from racing up to her room, and then the slam of Sinead's door. 'I just can't figure out how it all went wrong.'

'Anyhow, I don't even really *fancy* Travis!' Marina protested unconvincingly.

'Liar! Every girl in college fancies Travis.'

'OK, then, he is cute. And he's a great kisser.'

Upstairs, a door opened and footsteps shuffled into the bathroom. 'I heard that!' Sinead croaked.

'Big feet!' Frankie growled at Marina. 'Stick them both in your mouth, why don't you?'

They waited until they heard the flush of the toilet, then went and sat on the bottom of the stairs.

'Come down, Sinead!' Frankie implored. 'We need to talk to you.'

Sinead trailed slowly down. 'Ugh, my mouth feels like—'

'The interior of a camel's arse?' Frankie suggested, just to lighten the mood.

Marina laughed.

'Ouch, keep the noise down!' Hammers were bludgeoning away at the inside of Sinead's skull.

'Do you feel as bad as you look?' Frankie asked. 'More importantly, do you remember anything about last night?'

Marina watched as flickers of confused realisation passed across Sinead's face.

'It's OK, you didn't do it with anyone,' she assured her. 'But you *did* end up with my Rob, and I ended up with – erm – your Travis, and I'm sorry, sorry, sorry!'

Sinead sank to the floor and sat cross-legged. 'Please tell me that was a joke,' she begged.

'No, but listen, we were wrecked!' Marina insisted. 'It doesn't mean anything. It's just a little blip on the road to true happiness!'

'Who for?' Frankie inquired, relaxing now that the 'sorries' were bouncing off the walls.

'For Sinead and Travis, of course,' Marina explained. 'And you know whose fault this really was? It was stupid Rob's. He was supposed to – *ouch*!' She yelped as Frankie dug an elbow into her ribs.

'*Zzzzip!*' Frankie motioned for Marina to shut her mouth.

'Did I dance with Rob?' Sinead mumbled, thinking too slowly to pick any of this up. 'I did, didn't I? I can remember the smell of his jacket.'

'Old cow,' Frankie muttered. 'No, not you, Sinead – the jacket!'

'Oh my God!' Sinead groaned as the memories leaked back. Then 'Oh my God!' again as the front doorbell rang and she went slowly to look out of the bay window. She turned back to Marina and Frankie, her face white, her hands over her mouth. 'Daniella. Here. Now!'

'Oh no, your mother – bombsite! Clean up, quick!' Frankie yelped, leaping up from her cushion.

Marina ambled over to take a look. There was a tall, immaculate-looking woman standing on the doorstep. She had flicked-out, dark, bobbed hair, and was wearing a well-tailored, rose-pink and beige Chanel-style suit with cream, fringed edges on the jacket, and dusty-pink high-heels. 'Sinead, is that real Chanel?' she gasped. 'My God, she looks just like Audrey Hepburn!'

Brrring! went the doorbell again.

Sinead gulped and sprang into action. 'Coming!' she cried, as her numb fingers fumbled with the lock on the door.

'Fancy a spin?' Rob said to Travis, once he'd rebuilt his bike.

They sped along the mostly empty Sunday streets, stopped off at a couple of pubs, then sat on a bench by a canal. Neither of them mentioned the night before until late in the afternoon.

Then, 'You were dead right about the blonde one fancying me, mate,' Travis said smugly, as he checked out a few settings on his camera. 'Thanks.'

Rob leaned back against a brick wall warmed by the sun. He could feel the heat through his jacket. 'That's OK, mate,' he replied. 'I got the one in the blue dress.'

'Yeah, I saw that.' Travis crouched low to focus on some moss growing on the heavy timbers of the lock. Clever mechanism, this lock business, even if the technology was a couple of centuries old. 'Liked yours better than mine,' he confessed.

He'd stayed awake most of the night, remembering those slight shoulders, those arms, the way Sinead had danced with Rob but looked as if she was floating off through space. Weird – women didn't usually get under his skin this way. In fact, they *never* did!

'She was OK,' Rob acknowledged, yawning and looking at his watch. 'Too skinny for me, though.'

Travis zoomed in on the moss, the timber and the thin trickle of water oozing between two planks. 'Sinead's an Irish name. Is she Irish?'

'Dunno, didn't ask. Yeah, I reckon so.'

'Are you going to see her again?'

'Dunno. Yeah, well, I'll see her at work, won't I? Anyway, they only live across the square.'

You lay another finger on her and I'll tear your liver out! Travis thought. Then: *Get a grip, for God's sake! This is your best mate you're talking about. Your thick-skinned, beer-swilling, footie-obsessed best mate!*

Marina was in awe. She'd never seen anyone so perfect in the flesh as Daniella Harcourt.

Not that there *was* much flesh – just perfectly sculpted cheekbones, angles, and long, straight lines.

'Why are you back so soon?' Sinead asked, after Daniella had refused coffee and perched on the back of the futon in the living room.

'Sorry about the mess,' Frankie mumbled, scrambling to clear the floor space around Daniella's feet.

'I came back to see James, my English finance man. There's some stuff to sort out. It's a bore.' Rising above the chaos, Daniella opened her arms for a hug. 'Sinead, darling, you have dark circles under your eyes. Does that mean you've not been getting enough sleep?'

'Right,' Sinead admitted warily. Her mother had mentioned money for the first time in living memory. 'Is everything OK?' she asked.

'Perfect. Patrick's gone to New York for a few days, which leaves me free as a bird!'

Bird – yeah! Marina thought, developing a serious case of hero-worship. *Tiny, lightweight, able to spread its wings and soar . . .*

'We had a party here last night,' Frankie broke in. 'We're not usually this messy.'

Daniella bestowed a kind smile. 'Oh, students!' she laughed. 'If not now, then when?' She turned back to her daughter. 'Sinead, honey, I want to take you out to a sweet little restaurant that Patrick and I found last month. Go and get dressed while I make a few phone calls. Can you be ready in five minutes? There's a darling.'

There was something wrong. Sinead had a gut feeling that Daniella wouldn't fly back from Dublin so soon after she'd bought her the house on Walgrave Square unless there was a problem.

'How come you didn't go to New York with Patrick?' she asked, once they were installed in the most private corner of the trendy brasserie.

'Just coffee, please,' Daniella told the waiter. 'Darling, I don't have to trot along behind Patrick every step of the way, you know.'

'But you love New York.'

Daniella cocked her head to one side. End of conversation. 'So, how's fashion college?'

'Cool. We haven't done much practical work yet. It's mostly been meeting our tutors and a bit of theory.'

'What do you think of Tristan Fox?'

'Cool.'

'He's the reason I wanted you to come to Central. Of course, I've known Tristan for years. He did my wedding shoes when I married your father.'

'I know,' Sinead sighed. She decided that for once she would risk cutting through the crap. 'Mum, what's wrong?'

This time the head-cock didn't work and Daniella frowned at her coffee spoon. 'If you must know, Patrick and I have decided to take a break. Time apart, you know . . .'

'Oh, Mum, I'm sorry!' The brave face was only on the surface, Sinead knew. Yet another failed relationship. Deep down, her mother must be hurting like hell.

'Not half as sorry as I'll be if his American lawyers push for half the Dublin house!' Daniella gave a hollow laugh.

'He wouldn't!'

'He might,' she said. End of conversation. 'But anyway, darling, tell me more about Tristan. Is he up to speed with his Botox, or are the cracks beginning to show?'

'One glass of red wine contains one hundred and fifty calories,' Marina reminded herself the day after Daniella's surprise visit. She'd slotted the video of *Breakfast At Tiffany's* into a college TV and, with sketchbook in hand, got ready to scribble down design ideas from Audrey Hepburn's costumes.

How come skinny Audrey could risk eating breakfast? she wondered. *How many calories are in a croissant?*

'Are you talking to yourself?' Frankie asked, passing through the video library on her way to the jewellery workshop.

'Look at this!' Marina ordered. 'I swear, Sinead's mother is Audrey Hepburn's double!'

'Fantastic eyes,' Frankie noted, looking intently at the black-and-white screen. 'You know she had an eating disorder?'

'Who – Daniella?'

'No, stupid – Audrey Hepburn. She had to starve herself to stay that thin.'

'Well, I'm on a diet too,' Marina insisted.

'Since when?'

'Since this morning. I've got to get rid of these curves.'

'Whatever!' Frankie shrugged. Marina without curves would be like – well, Rob without his leather jacket.

'When I'm forty, I want to be like Daniella Harcourt!' Marina vowed. 'I mean, wasn't she so cool? Did you see the cut of that suit? And that ring – it was the biggest diamond I've ever seen!'

Frankie went on out of the library, paused at the door of the workshop, saw that there were three people already working in there, and did her panic-attack thing of walking right on by.

I've got to stop doing this! she told herself. *The others won't bite.*

'Cool party on Saturday,' Suzy Atkins said, passing Frankie in the corridor. 'If you're looking for Travis, I just saw him. He's in the darkroom.'

'Why would I be looking for Travis?' Frankie wanted to know.

Suzy's lips smiled but her eyes didn't. 'Oh come on, we all know you two are an item. You practically live out of each other's pockets.'

'No, we don't – and we aren't. Weren't you at the party on Saturday?'

'I left before it finished. Why?'

'Because it wasn't *me* snogging Travis in the garden at the end of the evening,' Frankie told her, then deliberately left it at that.

'Who was it then?' Suzy called after her, her voice rising off the top of the scale.

Silence from Frankie, who took delight in making it plain that she was headed straight for the Photography Department.

There was a red light on the darkroom door, so Frankie knocked.

'Give me a minute!' Travis called from inside, eventually opening the door a fraction, seeing Frankie and inviting her in.

'Come and look at these shots I took by the canal yesterday afternoon. See this one in the enlarger? I haven't got the contrast right yet, but what do you think of the composition?'

'Cool,' Frankie said. 'It looks kind of abstract, like a Rothko painting.'

'That's what I love about this process,' Travis enthused, adjusting the contrast, then getting ready to transfer the enlarged image onto a blank sheet of photographic paper. 'You start with nothing, and gradually the image appears – like a ghost at first, just faint shadows on white, then magically taking shape.'

Frankie nodded. She breathed in the sharp smell of the chemicals and watched Travis use tweezers to lift the newborn photograph out of the dish.

'Yeah, cool,' she agreed.

'You should do photography as a subsidiary subject next year,' Travis told her, dipping the picture into clean water.

'Listen, it's all I can do to get through the Jewellery course,' she admitted. And somehow, the small space of the darkroom, plus the dim green light, plus the fact that she felt she could trust Travis, led to Frankie telling him about the panic-attacks, and how she thought the other students were way more talented, cleverer and, well – more *everything* than she was.

'No way!' He sat her down on a stool and made her listen. 'Everybody feels that way the first couple of weeks, but you have to get over it.'

'Yeah, sorry. I sound pathetic.'

'No, you don't. But you've got to believe in yourself. No, that's not right. You've got to believe in what you *do*.'

'Like you and your photographs?' Once more, Frankie could hardly believe that a cool guy like Travis really seemed to care.

Travis nodded. 'Tell me the way you feel when you think about making a piece of jewellery. Go on, describe it to me.'

'OK . . . well I'm always looking around me, picking up objects – just ordinary things like pebbles or leaves – thinking, hey, that's a great shape, and drawing a sketch of it. I like colours and the texture of things, and I love the cold, smooth feel of silver and gold.'

'That sounds good.' Travis brought his stool closer. 'More!'

'I love gemstones – the way they shine and sparkle. Did you ever look at a moonstone, Travis? In some lights it's almost transparent, then you tilt it another way and it glows a pale, milky-blue, sometimes even pinky-red at a certain angle.'

'Wow!'

'Yeah, it is. I made this necklace last year with an enormous oval moonstone set in silver, and the silver was designed in an Art Deco style. I gave it to my mum for Christmas.'

'Sounds cool.'

'No, not totally. Not one hundred per cent. There were one or two details I could have done better.' Frankie knew she could have polished the stone to an even smoother finish, and she should have used a finer chain.

'So go and do it better!' Travis encouraged her. 'Get into that workshop and start working on that perfect design.'

Frankie pursed her lips. 'You're right,' she agreed.

'Go! Now!' Pulling her off the stool, he hustled her towards the door.

'Yeah, OK, but listen, I want to say thanks.'

'You said it. Go!'

'And I want to tell you something.' Again, the small, dark space, the green light and the urge to confide. *I'm doing you an enormous favour here, Sinead, if you did but know it!* Frankie thought. 'It's about Sinead.'

Travis knotted his eyebrows and stepped back.

'Don't look like that. It's nothing evil.'

'What then?' *Sinead in the blue dress, her arms wrapped around Rob's neck. Torture!*

'I don't know what Rob said to you, but he was meant to tell you that Sinead – well, Sinead – she likes *you*!'

Travis breathed out suddenly, as if he'd been punched in the stomach. '*Sinead?*' he asked.

'Yes. Marina told Rob to tell you. Why, what did Rob say?'

'That *Marina* fancied me,' Travis told her in a weak voice. 'She definitely acted that way on Saturday.'

'The lying, double-crossing toad!' Frankie cried, flinging open the darkroom door. 'Just wait until I get my hands on her!'

In fashion you had to work a couple of seasons ahead. Sinead was thinking spring – young virgins, old whites, antique pinks in layers, with mixed-up textures to give an image of romance.

She smoothed a length of white organdie onto the cutting-table, referred to her drawing of a gathered top, then started with the scissors. The crisp *snip* of the blades gave her a thrill. The top would have a skirt to match, with an asymmetric hem and a frill around the hips. The whole thing would be brought together by the palest pink cummerbund in satin, with a beaded, lace skull cap to top it off.

Shoes? she wondered, as she slid the cut organdie to one side. She'd seen some cream suede sandals by Martine Sitbon which she liked – high-heels, a retro design.

Sinead paused for a moment to glance out of the wide, tall window. The cutting room was at the top of the college building, so she looked out over tower blocks whose steel-and-glass frames gleamed in the weak sunlight. To the west was the green space of a park, to the east the river wound its way through the city.

'Music!' Sinead murmured, slotting in a favourite CD and selecting the best track. A moody, bluesy number, all about the dangers of opening up your heart.

And then back to the table, the smooth glide of scissors through metres of soft fabric, the vision becoming reality, the lovely, light innocence of her creation.

EIGHT

'It's zircon,' Rob told Marina. 'Looks like diamond but doesn't cost an arm and a leg.'

'So I could design this lapel brooch like the one in the Audrey Hepburn movie, and just fake it by using zircon?' Marina checked.

'Yeah, I'd say so.'

'Thanks!' Marina dazzled Rob with her twenty-four-carat smile. After the major cock-up that was Saturday night, she'd had to make a new plan and, so far, it seemed to be working. She'd found Rob in his tiny workroom stacked high with jewellery tools, lathes and polishers, and was attempting to stun him into submission, under the guise of picking his brains.

'But what do I know?' Rob mumbled, backtracking. 'I'm only the technician.'

'I should ask Claudia, right?' Nifty footwork was needed to keep Rob talking – if that's what you could call his monosyllabic growls. His voice came from deep within his throat, like Brando when he was method-acting. 'So you DJ in your spare time?'

Rob nodded and tried to reach past Marina for a box of zircons. The store room was so small that it brought them into physical contact. 'Sorry!' he mumbled.

Marina didn't mind. 'I'm not into garage and drum-and-bass,' she went on. 'I like glam rock and hip Fifties stuff – Sinatra, Sammy Davis Junior, that kind of thing . . . Oh, and Jamie Cullum's kinda cool.'

Glam rock – that figured. This was a girl who never went down the Seven-Eleven for a pint of milk without her lips fully glossed. So why was she putting it out for *him*? Surely he wasn't her type?

'D'you know Sammy Davis?' Marina picked up one of the clear, shiny stones from the box that Rob had handed to her.

'He was one of the Rat Pack,' Rob said. 'With Dean Martin, Sinatra and all that lot.'

'I *love* the Fifties – big skirts and high-heels; little Capri pants and white sneakers. Pure Grace Kelly. *So* glamorous!' Marina told Rob that she and Sinead spent every spare minute in vintage-clothing shops, and swore that she'd been born into the wrong decade.

'Sinatra was linked with the Mafia,' Rob pointed out.

'Yeah, and Marilyn had an affair with the President!' For Marina, nothing could dim the shine of that era.

'And she ended up alone, dead from a drugs overdose, with maybe the FBI involved.'

'You know about it!' Marina was pleasantly surprised. The conversation was going better than she'd expected. 'What d'you think – were the Kennedys behind Marilyn's death? Or the Mafia?'

'Marina!' Frankie's voice interrupted from outside the store room.

Rob spotted an escape route. 'She's in here!' he called, opening the door.

'Marina, you suck, you know that?' Frankie had come straight from Travis's darkroom to find the double-crosser. 'You lied to me. You didn't tell Rob that Sinead fancied Travis, you told him that *you* did!'

Marina whirled around to face Frankie. 'Puh-lease!' she scoffed. 'Does it *look* like I'm after Travis?'

'It did on Saturday night.' Frankie frowned, suddenly uncertain. But no way was Marina going to wriggle out of this.

'Tell her!' Marina yelled at Rob. Her temper, always on a short fuse, blew big time.

'Whoah!' Rob didn't fancy getting caught in the crossfire. He squeezed past Marina in a bid for freedom. 'Leave me out of this!'

'*Tell her!*' Marina insisted. 'What did I say to you before the party?'

'OK, OK – that *you* were after Travis,' Rob said breathlessly. 'Now, I'm out of here!' And he left, without locking his store room, thinking that riding a Kawasaki at a hundred and ten miles per hour down the motorway was far safer than having anything to do with a girl like Marina.

'Oh God, *typical!*' Marina groaned, deflating like a balloon. 'That guy has a brain the size of a peanut!'

But Frankie had got all the proof she needed. She was on a roll. 'How could you be so mean? Sinead's sharing her house with you and all you can do is think of yourself!'

'Oh, little Miss Perfect!' Marina retaliated. 'Don't tell me that your interest in Travis is totally – what's the word? – platonic!'

'What?' Frankie scowled.

'Go on, deny it – you know you want him!'

'I do not – and I wouldn't do that to Sinead, anyway. Not like you. You're a total selfish bitch!'

'Cat-fight!' Rob reported to Travis, when he found him in the coffee bar.

'Where?'

'Jewellery workroom. Your little mate Frankie and Marina the Killer-Shark.'

'What about?' Travis asked.

'You, mate,' Rob grinned smugly, biting into a Danish, before nearly choking on a pecan nut.

Marina was still ranting at Frankie. 'You're weird with guys!' she said. 'You play at being just friends, when you're really flirting. It's not fair – it's what's known as being a prick-tease!'

'Shut up!' Frankie yelled back. 'You're *obsessed* with sex. It's not all about wanting to get laid, you know.'

'You're so frigid that if a guy laid a finger on you, you'd cry rape!' Marina twisted the knife. 'You poor virgin. Talk about being "touched for the very first time" – you haven't even got to first base!'

'And you'd put out for the bin-man!' Frankie had had enough. 'I don't have to take this from you, Marina. I'm going home!'

'Make sure you tell Sinead that you're chasing Travis when you see her!' Marina flung after her. 'Might as well get the whole thing out in the open . . .'

Sinead was busy sketching. OK, so if the beaded cap came low down over the forehead, it would look more like a nineteen-twenties cloche . . . She redrew the lace headgear, envisaging it worn with long, tangled gypsy-girl locks. This outfit was about mixing styles, incorporating stuff she'd picked up in the market, achieving exactly the right combination of looks.

Five minutes earlier, her tutor had dropped by and suggested a slight alteration to the cap. 'It's an interesting idea,' Tristan had said. He'd checked on her cutting technique and then left without another word.

'*I open up my heart, you tear it apart . . .*' The track from her 'Loving You Is Hard' album played on. Sinead hummed the slow tune as she sketched.

'Hey.' Travis came into the light, airy space of the cutting room. He'd taken the lift up to the top floor straight from having coffee with Rob, hoping to find Sinead alone. OK, so it had taken him long enough to get to this point – to seek her out and say sorry about Marina and Saturday, could they delete that episode and maybe go out for a drink together – but here he was, ready to risk it.

With her back turned, Sinead didn't hear him.

Travis paused. This was a great moment – Sinead sat unaware, her head bent over her work, white fabric everywhere, the afternoon sun shining directly on her. He caught her profile – delicate features framed by short, blonde hair like a pale-gold halo.

At last something told Sinead that he was there. She let her pencil hover over the paper, then turned towards him.

Travis saw her mouth curve upwards at the corners in a surprised smile.

She let her eyes meet his. An electric moment, a missed heartbeat, a look that seemed to go on and on.

And then Marina burst through the door. 'God, Sinead!' she cried. 'I've just had the most enormous row with Frankie. The girl's gone crazy. You should hear what she's been saying about me!'

NINE

'Travis, this is me you're asking, remember?' Rob had to point out that he wasn't the world's expert on women. 'I don't do advice!'

'But how should I play this thing with Sinead?' Travis asked, sitting in the pub with his best mate, a couple of beers in front of them.

'Have you said anything to her yet?' Rob asked.

'No.'

'Has she said anything to you?'

Travis shook his head. Then: 'You don't mind, do you? I mean, after you and her – you know, Saturday night . . . 'cos if you do, I'll butt out.'

'No, mate, you go ahead. She's more your type, anyway.'

'I saw her earlier. She kind of looked at me, and I think there was a spark, but I'm not certain.' Travis was feeling a new emotion he couldn't quite put his finger on. It was forcing him to question every move he made.

'You make it sound like the ignition on an engine,' Rob said, grinning. Now a spark plug – *that* was something he *could* talk about.

'Yeah. Turn the key, spark up the engine!' Travis liked the comparison. 'Only, I'm not sure – do I have the right key?'

'Wow,' Rob said. 'This is way too friggin' deep. What happened to your usual technique of grabbing a girl round the waist and carrying her off?'

'That "me Tarzan, you Jane" thing is more up your street than mine.'

'Says the babe-magnet!' Rob had seen Travis at work. His friend had the looks of a rock star and a take-it-or-leave-it attitude that brought the girls flocking.

'Hmm.' Travis stared at his glass. 'I think this is different. But maybe it's not. I just don't know.'

'Well, I don't bloody know either,' Rob

concluded, finishing his pint. 'D'you fancy another beer?'

What could you read into a look? Sinead tried to tell herself that the glance in the cutting room meant nothing, but Marina wasn't helping.

'*Some enchanted evening . . .*' she'd crooned, waltzing round the room. '*You may see a stranger . . . You may see a stranger, a-cross a crowd-ed room . . .!*'

'Cut it out!' Sinead sighed, folding away her fabrics.

'I thought that's what *you* were doing – cutting it out! Y'know – *snip, snip.*' Marina's feeble joke fell flat, so she went on with her moan about Frankie. 'Honest to God, she really laid into me. Said I had sex on the brain!'

'So what did *you* say?' Sinead asked, noncommittal.

Marina shrugged. 'I called her a virgin.'

'You didn't!'

'I did. She is. Well, probably.'

'*So?*'

'So! She called me a nympho.'

This was going into nasty, dark corners, Sinead realised. She gave up and decided to let Frankie and Marina sort it out between themselves.

Back in Dublin, Sinead's mother texted, later that evening. P flying bck frm NY.

And, very late, when the house was dark and quiet, Sinead sat by her window, looking down on the square. So what *could* you read into a look? She'd glanced up from her work and Travis had been standing in the doorway, staring at her. So what?

He came up specially to see you.

Maybe.

For sure. He would have said something meaningful if Marina hadn't stormed in.

He does have beautiful eyes. And nice lips.

A good kisser, according to Marina.

Don't remind me.

From her window, Sinead caught glimpses of Number 45 through the beech trees. There was a light on in an upstairs window. What if that had been a one-off moment, back there in the cutting room? What if she never had another chance with Travis?

Life is what you make it, said the inner voice.

No, I think that life is what you get thrown at you, she argued. You only get one shot at someone like Travis. If you don't get him first time, you've missed your chance for good.

Suit yourself.

Friendship's safer, Sinead decided. That's what I'll work on.

Silence from the other voice.

She kicked off her slippers and slid into bed.

Claudia Brown let a week and a half of term-time go by before she summoned Frankie to her office.

'I don't get it,' she began. 'You came here to Central with the highest recommendations and one of the best entry portfolios I've ever seen from a kid straight out of school.'

Frankie chewed her bottom lip. She felt her shoulders go tense.

'I remember interviewing you last spring. I saw a girl with bags of confidence, an answer for everything, a big smile on her face. Then you come here and start the course, and what do I get? A little mouse without a word to say for herself.'

'Sorry,' Frankie mumbled.

'That's not the answer I want to hear.' Getting up from behind her desk, Claudia stood, a fierce five feet and two inches of intimidating challenge. 'For instance, why haven't I seen your finished designs for your first jewellery project, when all my other students have managed to hand them in on time? And why do I never see you in the workshop?'

Frankie shook her head.

'Talk to me. I won't bite.'

'I started my design,' Frankie mumbled. 'Then I didn't like it, so I started again.'

'Have you got it with you?'

Frankie nodded and took her sketchbook out of her bag. She flicked through page after page of rejected drawings until her tutor snatched the book away and stabbed her finger at an intricate sketch for a ring.

'Tell me about this,' Claudia demanded.

'It's designed as five separate rings that sit on

100

the finger together and make one wide band of different-coloured golds. The middle ring has a square setting with a turquoise stone.'

'And what's the idea behind it?'

'The sea,' Frankie told her. 'Waves, the colour of the ocean when the sun hits it. I was going to do a necklace and earrings as well. But no corny motifs like starfish or sea-horses.'

Claudia nodded. 'Good. I like it.'

Frankie took a deep breath. 'I'll do some more work on it then.'

'Yes, and hand it in by Friday. Now, how come you're not using the workshop? Come on, tell me straight.'

'No reason. I'm working at home.'

'Not good enough. You need to work with others, bounce ideas back and forth. Give me the real reason.'

'I try,' Frankie confessed. 'I build myself up every morning, but I get to the workshop door and my hands go all clammy and I get breathless and I just can't go in.'

Claudia looked at her. 'Panic-attack,' she diagnosed. 'Don't worry, I used to have them all the time. Couldn't face going to meet my clients, used to invent any old excuse. It went on for years.'

'Wow,' Frankie said quietly. She met the gaze of the small, hard-as-nails, world-famous jewellery designer, and couldn't imagine her crippled by nerves.

'Bad for business,' Claudia said. 'So I found myself an excellent hypnotherapist, and what d'you know, she cured me in a single session!'

Frankie's eyebrows almost vanished into her hairline.

Claudia's face relaxed into a rare smile as she handed Frankie back her sketchbook. 'It cost me a fortune, though. If I were you, I'd talk the problem through with a girlfriend, get them to come to the workshop with you a few times – see if that works.'

Frankie nodded and breathed again. 'Thanks.'

'Don't thank me, just do it and don't let me down. Ocean designs by Friday?' Claudia checked.

Already on her way out, Frankie turned and nodded.

'And no more Miss Mouse?'

Frankie smiled and shook her head quickly – then made an equally quick exit.

'. . . Claudia's really nice,' she told Travis at lunchtime. 'No, really – I mean it. She's cool.'

Believe this if you can! Marina typed to the world. **My brilliant tutor, Tristan Fox, has dared to criticise my style! He said my Hollywood glam image was 'so last year, darling'. I argued it was up to the minute, ironic, post-modernist retro, blah-blah. And anyway, how can the adored Marilyn ever be out of fashion?!**

I was in a seminar on major fashion influences of the late twentieth century, and I was reading out an essay I'd written about the movie, *Grease***, and how it had helped revive the Fifties fashion. I showed an image of Olivia Newton-John as Sandy, alongside the iconic image of Marilyn standing over a grate, her skirt blowing up, and that's when Tristan said I was too fixated on one particular period, and it showed in the way I dressed and acted! Dead personal. I mean, I don't tell him how wrong the early Cliff Richard look is on a guy of his age! Only kidding . . .**

It's hard, being picked on in public. Maybe I do ask for it, some people find me too in your face. But that's just the way I am. I was brought up that way.

So, if you can't stand the heat – get out of the kitchen, I hear you say. But what if the kitchen's all you've ever known?

Good job I was a girl – my mum wouldn't have known what to do with a boy. She loved picking out cute dresses for me and putting ribbons in my hair, even when every other mum was dressing their kids in Cloth-Kits dungarees and stripey T-shirts. Mum often made my clothes. That's how I learned to sew.

Anyway, enough already! Tomorrow I go into college in my halter-neck top and pencil skirt, and flaunt it, Fifties-style! Sinead's going to lend me a pair of shoes. Frankie's ignoring me. That makes three days now. Nightmare.

'At least he got us a decent model this time!' Marina whispered to Sinead, measuring with her pencil.

Life-drawing again, dammit! Frankie sighed. It was Friday – the day she had to hand in her ocean-themed designs to Claudia, and even Frankie thought that they were cool now. In fact, she felt positively excited about them, like she had when she'd talked to Travis about making jewellery. Still, she could have done without Jack Irvine's compulsory life-drawing module as part of her course!

Sinead made quick sketches of the young, black model. Jack had given them five minutes for each pose – just time to block in the girl's main features. Choosing a different-colour soft pastel for each drawing, Sinead was develop-ing a sheet of freely produced, flowing sketches.

'OK, thank you, Natalie!' Jack asked the girl to put on her robe, then went from student to student, commenting on their work.

'That's very strong, very dynamic,' he told Marina. 'These drawings have an element of surprise and originality.'

'What do you mean, surprise?' she quizzed.

'They don't belong to you. Or at least, to the image you project. I expected your work to be more lightweight: all fur coat and no knickers, as my Yorkshire grandmother used to say.'

'Is that good or bad?' Marina asked.

'Oh, good,' Jack assured her. 'Work hard for another twenty years and maybe I can make a proper artist of you.'

'Wow!' Sinead was impressed. Jack Irvine was another of Central's tutors who had an international reputation outside college. He'd studied with David Hockney and had recently mounted exhibitions in Barcelona and Prague.

For once, Marina was dumbstruck. Hers was the only work Jack picked out for comment before he went back to the model and arranged her in a new pose.

'This time, a photography student will come into the studio to take detailed pictures of the pose,' the tutor explained. 'He'll print off lots of copies, so that each of you will be able to take the photographs home to continue work on this piece. I'd like to see some painting developing from this study. The photographs will complement your sketches so that you can produce finished, well-considered work.'

Sinead was busy studying the new pose – Natalie was leaning back in a relaxed way, one arm over the back of the chair, her long hair braided into tiny corn-rows and held high on her head by a fuchsia-coloured silk scarf. She looked exotic and wonderful.

So when Travis turned out to be the photography student Jack had invited, Sinead hardly noticed. *Natalie's left shoulder is higher than her right,* she told herself. *From where I'm standing, it comes up to the same level as the bottom of her left ear . . .*

'Hey, Sinead, look who it is!' Frankie hissed.

'What? Oh!' Sinead's pastel crayon trembled over the fresh marks on the sheet. *Travis!*

'Rather too tentative,' Jack commented as he passed. 'Be bolder, like Marianna.'

'Marina,' Marina told him.

'Hey, Sinead,' Travis said in a low voice, when he stepped back from the model to check focuses and apertures. He saw that she'd smudged her cheek with cobalt-blue pastel, and had to check an irresistible urge to gently wipe it clean with his thumb.

'Hey,' she breathed back. She saw where his gaze was directed, and self-consciously rubbed her face with the back of her hand.

Say something to him! Frankie willed Sinead to make a move.

Why are you hanging back? Marina thought.

As if she could mind-read, Sinead plunged ahead. She backed away from her drawing board, taking Travis into a quiet corner. 'I just wanted to say, I'm sorry you walked into that bitchy stuff about Frankie and Marina the other day,' she began, sounding unbelievably prim. She kicked herself.

'Hey, no problem,' he told her. *Lame, lame, lame!* Maybe the chemistry was wrong after all. Maybe this was just going to be a straight friendship.

Bang! Someone's board fell from their easel, crashing onto the floor.

Sinead jumped a mile. 'Sorry!' she murmured.

The crash jolted Travis through the shyness barrier. 'I've finished here, why don't we go for a coffee?' he said, suddenly.

'When?'

'Now.'

'I can't. I'm in the middle of a class.'

'Come anyway.'

Go! Marina and Frankie willed from a distance.

Which was how Sinead came to be drinking lattes with Travis when her phone vibrated and a text message came through from Daniella. Dn't gt 2 cosy in Wlgrve Sq, sweetie. I may hve 2 sell 2 pay my debts!

TEN

'She told you in a *text message*?' Frankie was horrified.

'Oh my God!' Marina wailed. 'It's so not fair!'

The news from Daniella had ruined everything. Sinead had kept up a front for Travis in the coffee bar, but she'd hardly been listening to a word he said.

'Sorry about Saturday,' he'd mumbled. 'None of that stuff with Marina was meant to happen.'

'No problem.'

'No, I mean it. It was a big foul-up. I don't always go round picking up random women at parties – especially, well, y'know.'

'Yeah.' She'd nodded. Then, 'Listen, Travis,

I'm really sorry, but I've just had a message. I've got to go. See you.'

And she'd left without asking what he'd been trying to say when he'd stumbled over the "especially, well, y'know" part of his pre-rehearsed speech.

Who knows how she got through the rest of the day; going to her class with Tristan Fox and working all afternoon in the cutting room before meeting up with Marina and Frankie back home that evening.

I'll get them both together and tell them, she decided, wandering aimlessly from room to room, before they got in.

'Hey, Sinead!' Frankie had burst through the door beaming from ear to ear. 'Guess what? I handed in the design for my jewellery project. I finally did it! And I spent the afternoon in the college workshop. Progress or what!'

'Jeez, these shoes are *killing* me!' Marina had collapsed onto the futon. 'So, Sinead, how did the coffee with Travis work out?'

'Daniella may have to sell the house. This house.' Sinead ignored Marina and came straight out with the bad news. There was no good way to do it. But she hadn't expected tears to come to her eyes, or a shake in her voice.

She told them about the text, and the reasons behind it.

'Daniella has split from Patrick,' she explained. 'I called her at one o'clock. She couldn't really talk because she was out having lunch, but she did tell me that much.'

'And Patrick is . . . ?' Marina asked.

'The guy from New York. Daniella's been in a relationship with him for about two years, but it hasn't worked out. He flew back to see her a couple of days ago, and broke the news that he had someone else. End of story.'

'Bummer,' Frankie said, quietly. 'What was he like, this Patrick?'

Sinead shrugged. She stood with her back to the window, surrounded by a pinky-orange glow from the streetlight. 'Daniella liked him.'

'But you didn't?' Marina guessed. 'So how come them splitting up means your mum has to sell this place?'

'*Might* have to!' Sinead stressed. 'Nothing's definite, but Patrick's got himself a smart lawyer. They're working out a deal to split the value of the Dublin house. Daniella put it in both their names when she bought it, and now he wants half. She'd rather sell this place to pay him off than risk losing it. She loves that house. It overlooks the park.'

'No way would I give this Patrick guy half! She should get herself an even smarter lawyer,' Frankie pointed out.

'Oh, she will,' Sinead said. Her mother wasn't stupid.

'How did she sound when you spoke to her?' Marina wanted to know.

'OK. Like I said, she couldn't really talk.' Sinead wasn't telling the others the whole conversation.

'. . . Darling, it's been on the cards for almost a year now. Things haven't been right between Patrick and me, and the money's become a bit of a problem recently.'

Then why did you buy me this place? Sinead had to bite her tongue to stop herself asking. And she hadn't been prepared for Danielle's second bombshell.

'And listen, darling – if Patrick wins this

stupid fight over the Dublin house, I might have to take you out of college as well as selling the student house. It's the fees, and the cost of keeping you over there – well, I simply won't be able to afford it!'

'So, anyway.' Frankie was thinking ahead. 'If it turns out that Daniella has to sell Walgrave Square, the three of us just go to the housing office and find ourselves a new place to rent. It might not be as cool as this house, but hey, so what! It'll be a roof over our heads – end of problem!'

Marina nodded. 'The three of us.'

'So you two are talking again?' Sinead asked, to change the subject. She didn't want to mention that she might have to ditch her course. That bit hurt too much even to think about.

Daniella made a habit of messing with her life – sometimes she felt like a stormy wind was blowing her this way and that. But you got used to it, and tried to hang onto one solid thing to keep you sane. In this case, that was her new friendship with Frankie and Marina. And she was damned if Daniella was going to screw that up.

Marina looked up from the sofa at Frankie, who was leaning against the doorpost. Frankie rolled her eyes.

'I guess so,' they said in unison.

'We're so over that stupid fight!' Marina insisted.

'Yeah, we three stick together!' Frankie agreed.

Sinead took a deep breath. 'Come on, let's forget about Daniella and go down the pub!'

Marina, Frankie and Sinead were on the dance floor. It was midnight and they'd moved on from The Alex to Strawberry Fields, the most happening club in town.

The music boomed, and the lights zapped, swung and zoomed in on people dancing on balconies, platforms and in the big central well. On the tiny stage, six professional dancers twisted and glittered in front of the funky DJ.

'This place is packed!' Marina complained between tracks. 'I need a drink.'

'Me too.' Frankie squeezed between steaming bodies towards the nearest bar. 'Water!'

she demanded, handing a bottle each to Marina and Sinead.

They found a corner of space on a staircase between two dance floors, sank down onto the metal steps and drank.

'Dance?' a bloke asked Frankie, before she'd even parked herself. She took a swig of water and shot off with him.

'Marina!' A girl from college recognised her. 'I was just talking to Suzy about you!'

'Suzy who?' Lucy Denton wasn't really Marina's favourite fellow student, but if people were discussing her, she needed to know.

'Suzy Atkins, in the second year.' Sitting in the gap left by Frankie, Lucy settled in for a goss. 'She reckons you should back off from Rob Evans. Suzy had a thing going with Travis, so she knows about Rob. Says he's bad news.'

Sinead heard snatches of this conversation, preferred not to, so shrugged and got up. 'See you later,' she told Marina.

She went to the loo, checked her hair in the mirror and suddenly fell out of the mood for dancing. *Pop!* The Friday night balloon had burst. Now all she wanted to do was go home.

'Get a taxi!' Marina warned, when Sinead told her she was leaving. 'Hey, did you know that Suzy had a fling with Rob as well as Travis? Lucy says Rob's a footie-dependent saddo! He needs to go to FFA.'

'What's that?'

'Football Fanatics Anonymous.'

Sinead grinned. 'So what's new?'

'I know. But he's still the ultimate challenge!'

'Dummy!' Sinead smiled, waving as she went.

'Get a cab!' Marina said again, then headed for the dance floor to find Frankie.

Outside in the cold night air, Sinead tried to take Marina's advice. She stood on the pavement, watching a couple get into the only cab standing at the kerb, then huddled back against the wall to wait for another. There were spots of rain in the air. Across the street, the window of the all-night pizza café was framed by red and green neon strips.

'Want a ride?' a guy called to Sinead from a car that had pulled up nearby.

A second, leering passenger in the back seat

wound down his window and hung out, arms outstretched. 'Hey, babe!' he slobbered.

'Get lost,' Sinead muttered. *Come on, taxi, get me out of here!*

'Yeah, beat it!' Travis butted in, coming up alongside Sinead and looking as though he'd like to kick the guys' heads in.

The car drove off.

'Hey!' Sinead said. 'Where did *you* come from?'

'I followed you out.' Travis stood without a jacket, hands in pockets.

'Why? Are you my knight in shining armour?'

'I didn't like the idea of you leaving alone.'

'I can take care of myself. Anyway, I didn't see you in there.'

'It's pretty packed,' Travis said. He'd spotted a cab winding its way through the traffic towards them. 'Why did you leave?'

'No reason.'

She was blanking him, pushing him away, just like she had when she'd got Daniella's text message earlier that day.

Travis could tell when he wasn't wanted.

'Here's a cab,' he muttered.

The taxi slid through the last set of red lights and pulled up at the kerb.

'We could walk home,' Sinead suggested suddenly, as if from nowhere.

'In the rain?' OK, this was confusing. One second he got a red light from Sinead, the next a green!

'I don't mind getting wet.'

'Me neither.'

Travis set off up the hill, a little bit ahead of Sinead. Then he turned to wait for her.

'It's these shoes,' she explained.

'I heard you might have to leave your house,' he said, taking her hand.

His hand felt big and warm. 'Who told you?'

'Frankie. I saw her earlier, in The Alex. We had a chat.'

'Did she say *why* we might move?'

'Nope. But you only just moved in. So how come?'

'It's complicated,' she sighed.

And there she was, blocking him out again, not giving anything away. But she looked so cool in her short white dress, the two big silver-

119

and-blue butterfly brooches holding its straps in place, her spiky high-heels bringing her up to his height, he couldn't let her go. He stopped at the kerb to wait for the green man. 'You're getting wet.'

'It's not far now. Listen, I don't want to move from the square. It's just stuff to do with my mum.'

'Yeah, well, if it means anything, I don't want you to move either.'

Sinead looked at him. 'No one to fix your washing machine?'

'Huh.' He pulled her away from the road as a car swept through a puddle.

'Daniella – that's my mother – has a few money things to sort out. She's just split from her partner. Not my dad – he's long gone. But it looks like it could turn nasty.' *Hey, blabbermouth!* She pulled herself up short, then set off across the street ahead of Travis.

'I'm sorry,' he said. Meaning, about everything. He caught her up and put his arm around her shoulder.

'Don't worry, I'm not going to blub all over your T-shirt!'

He ran ahead and, walking backwards, threw his arms wide. 'Feel free!'

'OK, well, get this!' Sinead said. She was laughing and wanting to cry at the same time. Over Travis's shoulders she could see the bare branches of the beech trees in the centre of Walgrave Square. 'Not only might my wonderful, stupid, crazy mother make me move house, but she's threatening to take me out of college, period!'

Travis grew serious and walked her in amongst the trees. The silver-grey trunks were dark with rain, the branches letting cold drops fall.

'I've let you get inside my head,' he confessed. 'You're in there, messing up the stuff I'm supposed to do with my life. I can't get you out of my mind.'

'Do you want to?' she asked. She gave in to the feel of his arm around her waist, the warmth of him, as his face drew close to hers.

'No,' he said.

'I'm not easy to be with,' she warned.

'Says who?'

'People. I have hang-ups.'

121

Travis put his lips against her cheek. 'Like what?'

'Like whether I can trust you. Whether we would be better just as friends.'

He kissed her on the lips in answer. Her skin and hair were wet from the rain. Then her arms were around his neck and she was kissing him back.

ELEVEN

'God, pulling Rob is worse than pulling teeth!' Marina bleated.

Frankie laughed. 'I like it! This is history in the making – the first time *ever* a guy has ignored your charms!'

They were still dancing in the crush of the club, antennae raised for hunky guys.

'I've tried everything I know,' Marina admitted. 'The cleavage, the hip-wiggles, the eyelash-flutter. And what does he do? Gives me the latest Premiership positions of Arsenal and Chelsea.'

'Maybe he's in denial,' Frankie suggested, ignoring the wave of a guy she'd danced with earlier. He'd done an embarrassing break-dance routine, so Frankie had brushed him off, but he'd been stalking her around the club ever since. 'Rob looks like the type who'd refuse to admit that love could ever rate above kicking a leather ball around a square of turf.'

'Denial?' Marina considered this.

'Yeah, that would be his mother's fault. She most likely overprotected him when he was a little kid, bossed him around too much, that kind of thing. Now Rob thinks that we're all like his mum, so psychologically he has to run away and hide from any woman who shows an interest in him.'

'Wow.'

'You're impressed? Me too. I did Psychology A Level.'

As the music thudded and a deep voice hammered out lyrics, Marina spread her hands in bewilderment. 'Excuse me – but how could I *possibly* remind Rob of his mother?'

The look of horror on Marina's face made Frankie break out in giggles, so she was off-guard when Break-Dance Man broke in between her and Marina. He twitched and elbowed Marina out of the way and, when

Frankie had stopped laughing, there he was, boogying like crazy.

'Nice body, pity about the dancing!' Marina mouthed, as she backed off. She went on a Rob-hunt and found him just where she expected, close to the bar.

'Where's Travis?' she began. Not a great conversational gambit, but it would have to do.

Rob shrugged.

'I've been thinking about those zircon stones you told me about,' she lied. 'I went ahead and designed the brooch. Now all I have to do is make it – with your help, naturally!'

'Hmm.'

'Yeah, you're right. That's work stuff – boring!'

'Drink?' Rob asked, like Pavlov's dog. Stand at bar – talk – offer to buy drink. Conditioned response.

Wow, progress! Marina nodded, then saw the barman bring the shutters down. 'Too late. They're closed.'

'Time for bed,' Rob said in a dozy voice, sounding like he'd overdone it. He glanced round, failed to spot Travis, so said to Marina,

'You coming?' Then he frowned. Someone like her was bound to take that the wrong way.

'Yes – no, hang on a second!' Marina rushed to find Frankie.

'Guess what! You're not going to believe this, but Rob just offered to walk me home!'

'Go for it,' Frankie told her, still fending off Break-Dance Man and wondering how come she'd ended up with Mr Geek while Marina was on a roll with Rob.

The DJ had played his last track, the club was rapidly emptying.

'You'll be OK?' Marina checked.

'Don't worry, I'll look after her,' the guy promised.

With her back to him, Frankie made a face at Marina. 'This is Lee,' she grunted. 'Lee – Marina.'

'Hi. So you'll be OK?'

'Go, before Rob changes his mind!' Frankie insisted.

Yeah, she'd taken it the wrong way. Rob saw

the killer look in Marina's eye as she headed back towards him. She thought a walk home meant they were practically engaged.

'It's raining,' he muttered, as they made it outside.

Marina hopped neatly over a puddle. She pictured Gene Kelly singing in the rain: *'What a glor-ious feel-ing – I'm ha-ppy again!'*

Jeez, the girl was nuts. She was grinning about the rain, grabbing his hand and half-dancing up the hill.

'It's OK, I can catch a cab,' Frankie told Lee. Her hands felt sticky and her heart was thudding, like it always did around boys.

But there was a queue a mile long outside the club.

'I'll walk you,' he insisted.

'You don't need to come all the way.' Ahead of them, Frankie kept Marina and Rob in her sights. Lee was turning into Velcro-Man, and the last thing Frankie wanted was for him to know where she lived. So, when they reached the top of the hill, she planned to say goodbye and leg it.

OK, so he wasn't bad-looking. In fact, he had good taste in shirts and a not unattractive, kind of little-boy-lost face. It was just the dorky dancing that was a turn-off.

'So, what do you study?' Lee asked eagerly. 'I bet it's something artistic. You look like someone who's into art.'

'When's your next gig?' Marina asked Rob. She couldn't do football or motorbikes, but she could do music.

'Sunday,' he told her.

'Where?'

'Down The Alex.'

'Cool.' The rain was stopping, so at least her hair wouldn't get totally wrecked.

OK, maybe Marina wasn't so scary. She looked more human with the rain in her hair and on her face.

'My brother DJs back home. He's sixteen.'

'That's the age I started. I did it full-time for a couple of years.'

'Then you got a proper job,' Marina said. *Wow, she and Rob were having a real conversation!* 'But you must always have been into music?'

'I played bass guitar in a band for a bit.'

'Then what happened?'

'We weren't into serious rehearsing, so we could only ever play the same five numbers. And Saturdays were out for me; I had footie then.'

'Did you play, or just watch?'

'Played – inter-schools cups, five-a-side . . . you name it, I played it.'

'I don't know the first thing about football,' Marina admitted. 'Yeah, yeah – so why doesn't *that* surprise you?'

'Here,' Rob said, taking off his jacket impulsively and carefully draping it around her shoulders.

Here they were, then – at the top of the hill. Frankie put on her best matey smile and told Lee she'd be fine from here.

'Can't I walk you to your door?'

'No, honestly, I'm fine.' She saw the hurt look, like he'd been kicked in the teeth, and felt lousy. But that didn't mean she was gonna kiss him. 'Give me your phone,' she said, then typed in her number. 'Text me, OK?'

'Cool,' Lee said, quietly. He didn't try to make a move on her.

'See you.'

'See you.'

And she left Little-Boy Lee standing on the edge of Walgrave Square.

'You gave me your jacket!' Marina said with a half-gasp, half-giggle. 'That's so cool!'

'It's raining. You looked cold.' Rob had walked Marina right to the gate of Number 13. His heavy jacket hung from her shoulders, hiding the strappy top but still letting him see plenty of curvy hip and shiny, black trouser.

She opened the gate. Now came the awkward bit.

'Come in for coffee,' she offered.

Rob saw a light on in a downstairs room and shook his head. 'I'd best get back.'

Don't push it! Marina told herself, for once in her life. 'OK. Thanks.' She smiled, then took off the jacket and handed it to him.

'Thanks.' He hovered by the front door.

She was still smiling, hesitating. Hovering and hesitating. *This is weird!* she thought.

Then the gate latch clicked and Frankie came rushing up the path. 'Oh for God's sake, Rob, just snog her and get on with it!' she said, as she passed.

'Thank the Lord!' Frankie was perched on the futon, dunking chocolate-chip cookies into her mug of coffee, listening to Sinead. 'At last everyone's snogging the right people!'

'I hate that word,' Sinead protested. '"Snogging." It sounds like frogs and snails, all slimy.'

'So what would you call what Marina is currently doing with Rob on our top step?'

Sinead took a peek through the blind at Marina and Rob, locked in each other's arms, lips glued. 'Yeah, that's snogging,' she admitted.

'What about you and Travis then?'

'*That* was kissing!' Sinead insisted, then laughed. She was still floating on cloud nine, a whole hour after she and Travis had said a long goodnight.

'So, tell me! C'mon, 'fess up!' Frankie was beginning to regret she'd ever asked, yet curiosity drove her on.

'He's so sweet,' Sinead murmured, a smile enveloping her whole face.

'Not enough. Gimme more.'

'I can talk to him. He listens.'

'Yep, that's a good start.' *I go along with that – Travis is a great listener!*

'He's got a really good sense of humour.'

'Hmm.' *Yeah, he makes me laugh too.*

'And he's drop-dead gorgeous.'

'Better!' *Oh my God, she's really into him, and it's all down to me!* But Frankie knew she had to let Sinead burble on without giving anything away.

'No, seriously, Frankie, I fancy the pants off him – but so do a zillion other girls. That's the problem.'

'Not a problem, unless he fancies the pants off the competition as well as you.'

'*If* he fancies me.'

'Oh, come off it, Sinead, everyone who isn't blind fancies you! Anyway, you snogged him, didn't you? He was obviously pretty enthusiastic.'

'Yeah, it was nice,' Sinead admitted. 'But honestly it took me totally by surprise. He actually followed me out of the club and brought me home. I was doing my "don't touch me!" routine, and then suddenly we were kissing!'

'Cool.' Frankie gulped hard, then dunked a cookie too deep and saw half of it crumble and sink to the bottom of her mug.

At the same time, the front door opened and Marina sailed in. 'Result!' she announced, with a grin like the Cheshire cat's.

'We know!' Frankie laughed.

'Gory details, please!' Sinead demanded.

'He's gorgeous!' Collapsing on the sofa beside Frankie, Marina began a blow-by-blow account. 'He actually talked to me in words of more than one syllable. He plays guitar. He was in a band.'

'OK, fast-forward to the clinch!' Frankie demanded, feeling the odd one out as per usual. She fished out soggy lumps of cookie with her spoon.

'It was cool!' Marina grinned. 'He's kind of shy, but that's fine by me.'

'Is that it?' Sinead pretended to be disappointed.

'That's it for now,' Marina insisted, still revelling in the sensation of being up close with Rob the unpullable. She turned to Frankie. 'So, how about you and Break-Dance Man?'

'Oh, me,' Frankie shrugged. 'His name's Lee. He dances like a dork. That'd be *nul points* from the British judge.'

Travis was still up, watching Sky, when Rob battered on the front door and he went to open it.

'Forgot my bloody key,' Rob grunted.

Travis glanced across the square to see lights still on at Number 13.

'What happened to you?' Rob asked, slumping down in Travis's chair.

'I left early, at about one.' *With Sinead, the girl of my dreams. We talked. We kissed.*

'Man, what's with you? There was a whole hour's drinking time left.'

Travis shrugged. 'I didn't feel like staying. I walked back.'

'Me too.' *With Marina, and I didn't get eaten alive! I actually talked to her. I'm even thinking of asking her out.*

134

'By yourself?' Travis asked.

'. . . Yeah. You?'

'. . . Yeah.'

Rob flicked the buttons on the remote until he found a football game.

'I'm knackered,' Travis yawned. 'I'm gonna crash.'

TWELVE

Can I c u? Lee texted Frankie early on Saturday morning.

Too needy, she decided, quickly erasing the message.

Rob and I finally got together, Marina blogged. **He's so not my type. I like guys in designer shirts who do romantic stuff like buying red roses and taking you to Paris for the weekend. Rob isn't witty, he doesn't do compliments and he's addicted to football – yuck! But he's under my skin.**

It's probably something to do with opposites attracting, like in physics. Isn't there some law, to do with Newton and the apple? Or is that something else?

I mean, he's my total opposite. But underneath the macho stuff, I reckon he's pretty complicated. Frankie thinks he's scared of women.

What's to be scared of?

Moi? I wouldn't hurt a fly!

If anything, *I'm* scared of *him*! Not scared, exactly. It's that animal thing – he's six-feet two of solid muscle, with stubble, pecs and a six-pack. Whoah, just thinking about it gives me goosebumps!

Now, the thing is, will he ask me out on a real date? And how long do I give him to make the next move? If he *doesn't* do it, should I? Like I tell Sinead, this *is* the twenty-first century. The girl is allowed to make the first move. Only, with Rob it wouldn't work. That's my guess, anyway. So I just have to sit here and wait.

No, get real. This is Marina Kent talking! Since when did I sit around waiting? It's Saturday. Shopping. Getting glammed up. Going out . . . See ya!

'What's with this fashion thing?' Travis asked

Sinead. He watched her leaf eagerly through *Vogue*, then *Harpers* in the newsagent's.

'What d'you mean, "what's with this fashion thing?"?' She glanced up at him. 'That's like me saying to you, "what's with the photography thing?"?'

'*Whoo*, touchy!'

'Well, you wouldn't ask me that question if I was into something like molecular science or Old Icelandic.'

'Yeah, I would. I'd want to know what makes you tick.'

Sinead nodded. 'OK, sorry, you're right. I'm touchy. Look at us, we're having our first row and we haven't even been out on a date yet.'

'Isn't this a date?' Travis had knocked on the door of Number 13 to ask Sinead if she was going into college.

'It's Saturday!' Marina had pointed out, swishing past him and down the path, armed with a frightening array of credit cards.

'Yeah, I'm coming,' Sinead had told him. 'I have to sew pearl beads onto a hat I'm making. It's going to take for ever.'

So they'd walked into town together, stopped for coffee, then strolled into the newsagent's.

'This doesn't count,' Sinead said, putting the mags back in the rack. 'Dates have low lighting, candles, wine, music . . . OK, I'm kidding!'

'Good. I don't do candles.'

Out in the street, Travis asked the same question again. 'So, why fashion?'

'For the glamour,' Sinead said, glancing at the blank-eyed mannequins in every shop window. 'And because fashion is dressing up, putting on an act, hiding who you really are.'

'Hiding?'

'Yeah.'

'Huh. I thought it was about making people look at you.' He pictured supermodels on the catwalk, strutting their stuff, celebs posing for the camera in their Versace dresses.

'No, it's about making people look at the outside so they ignore the inside. It's like a diversion, a disguise.' Sinead had thought this through over the years, watching Daniella do just that. 'They stare at your French manicure and spend time wondering where you had

139

your hair done, which lets you get on quietly with your latest nervous breakdown.'

'Huh.' Travis said again, pushing through the swing-doors of the college entrance. 'That sucks.'

Sinead decided it was time to lighten up. 'OK, it does. How about, I do fashion because I love fabrics, colour, texture . . .'

'Better.'

'. . . And I'm fascinated by what people wore two hundred years ago, fifty years ago, five hundred years ago . . .'

'Got it.'

'. . . And by embroidery and dyes, weaving and knitting . . .'

'Stop!' he begged. 'Sorry I asked. Listen, I developed those shots I took in the life-drawing class. D'you want to come and take a look?'

All Saturday, Marina shopped.

Frankie stayed in bed until midday. When she staggered to the bedroom window to open the blind, she spotted Rob squatting on the pavement outside Number 45, bits of bike engine spread out on an oily cloth.

Meanwhile, Travis mixed chemicals and made pictures. Sinead sewed rows of tiny pearl beads.

Have bought cool pair of cut-offs to wear with my stiletto black boots, Marina texted Frankie.

Can I c u? Lee texted a second time.

Frankie switched off her phone, pulled down the blind and went back to bed.

'Coffee?' At lunchtime, Travis came up to the sewing room and dragged Sinead out for a break.

In the afternoon, Marina made a momentous decision. 'I want to change my look!' she announced to the senior stylist at Toni and Guy. 'This is a major, major thing for me. Make me more urban chic, less Hollywood. Go ahead, just do it!'

'Sure?' the stylist double-checked.

Marina gritted her teeth and sat in the white-leather and chrome chair like a man on Death Row.

Rob cleaned his spark plugs, then went inside to catch the latest scores.

At half-three Frankie finally crawled out of bed. She hit the chocolate-chip cookies.

'Cool!' Sinead told Travis, at the end of the day.

He'd printed poster-size images of close-ups of a piece of silver lace she'd shown him. The leaf detail was worked over on the computer in Photoshop to highlight the pixels and make it look like a Pointillist painting – all blurry dots.

'I'd like to digitally print that onto silk,' she decided.

'Hey, we're a team!' he grinned.

Can I c u? Lee texted yet again.

No, Frankie texted back.

'Hey, Rob, what d'you think?' Marina burst into Number 45 with her expensive new urban chic hairdo.

'Uh?' Eyes glued to the screen, Rob clocked that Man United had lost – *yeah!*

'What d'you think?' She gave him a twirl.

He glanced round. 'What?'

'My hair, dummy! D'you like it?'

'Yeah, great.' Liverpool had beaten Wolves at Molyneux, Newcastle were drawing one-all with Chelsea.

'Rob Evans, you're the rudest, most ignorant apeman in the whole freaking world!' Marina sighed, collapsing onto his lap, turning his face towards hers and delivering an enormous kiss on the lips.

'I thought you didn't do candles,' Sinead smiled.

She'd gone home from college, got changed into a cream bandeau top and jeans, then gone across the square to Travis's place.

Rob was out, the TV turned off and two chunky candles stood flickering on the coffee table.

'You look fantastic.' *It was the shoulders,* Travis decided. *Yeah, definitely the shoulders. Then again, it was the whole package.*

Sinead watched as he put on a CD. 'Candles . . . music . . .' She ticked off items on her fingertips.

'Wine!' He produced an open bottle of red, plus two glasses.

'Oh my God, I'm dating Mr Romantic!' she laughed. 'Where are the chocolates?'

'Hey, this isn't funny!' He pretended to sulk. 'I went to a lot of trouble to fix this!'

So she took the glasses from him and they smooched to the music. 'I can't believe this is happening!' she whispered.

'Yeah!'

'It *is* happening, isn't it?'

'No, it's probably a dream.'

'Oh God, are we going to wake up?'

'No.' He breathed her in, blended with her movements. The dance degenerated to a shuffle, then a collapse onto the sofa.

'Wine!' Sinead sighed, surfacing for breath.

'He didn't even notice my hair!' Marina told Frankie. 'I mean, how can that be?'

'Men!' Frankie shrugged.

'And guess what, he's gone to stay with a

mate in Manchester tonight, so he can go to some stupid rally thing tomorrow morning!'

'Rat!'

'He said he'd fixed to go ages ago and he couldn't back out.'

'Louse!' Frankie drew on eyeliner and brushed on lip-gloss.

'But I'm going to watch him DJ at The Alex tomorrow night.' Marina checked her cut-offs and boots, which she'd teamed with a black lace top.

'You sure you're not turning yourself into a doormat?' Frankie challenged.

'Says the fridge-freezer, Frankie McLerran!'

'Meaning?' Frankie ran a hand through her dark mane to roughen up the effect.

'Meaning, you give guys the biggest cold-shoulder. Look at that one in the club last night: Lee.'

'What about him?'

'You froze him out. There must be a name for what you've got – boyfriend-phobia or something.'

Frankie gave Marina a confused, wounded look that stopped Marina stone-dead. Then she

145

sprang back. 'Doormat! C'mon, let's go before I give you a seriously big sock in the jaw!'

'D'you want to go out or stay in?' Travis asked.

'Stay in.' Sinead felt totally warm and cosy with Travis, as if they'd been going out for ever, instead of just nineteen hours and twenty-one minutes.

'Fancy a coffee, or anything?'

'What's the "anything"?'

'Kiss?' he suggested, hopefully.

She kissed him. 'What else?'

'Come upstairs to my room?'

Sinead hesitated, watching the two candles on the table flicker and die.

'No, it's OK. It's too soon,' he agreed, hollowly.

She held her breath.

'Anyhow, my room's a wreck. I haven't made the bed for a week.'

'Your planning for the evening didn't get that far, then?'

'You're joking! I still can't believe you're actually here.'

'Me neither.' They sat in the dark, until she

said, 'I suppose we could go up.'

On the stairs there was man-clutter – old newspapers, a bike helmet, odd socks. And Travis hadn't lied about his room. Sinead saw the duvet bundled to the bottom of the bed, dead shirts and jeans on the floor. And there was a triangular traffic sign screwed to the wall above the bed, which read 'Give Way', and underneath a fluorescent strip from a theatre billboard, pasted to the wooden bedhead, saying 'Tonight!' in bold, black capitals.

'"Give Way Tonight!" Mr Smooth!' she laughed. The stupid sign sent her reeling, giggling, falling helplessly head over heels in love.

THIRTEEN

'Where's Sinead?' Frankie croaked. It was unbearably early on Sunday morning – something like eleven-thirty.

Marina was downstairs, dressed in jogging bottoms and a halter-neck, doing a work-out routine to a video. The thumps and groans had woken Frankie from a deep, drunken slumber.

'In bed?' Marina suggested. Hands behind head. Sit-up once, twice, three times. *Ugh-ugh*.

'Not in her own bed,' Frankie reported. 'It's not been slept in.'

Raise right leg without bending knee, hold, let it drop. *Ugh*. 'Passed out on front-room sofa?'

Frankie went to check. 'Nope.' Then she picked up her phone from the kitchen table: 1 message received.

Raise left leg without bending, hold – one, two, three, four, five. Let it drop. *Ouch!*

Frankie pressed 'read'.

Am at T's – S

'Ohmigod!' Frankie flopped down on the futon and tried to take in what she'd just read.

'What happened? Is it World War Three?' Marina stared at Frankie's face. 'Come on, tell me!'

'It's Sinead!' Frankie quavered.

'Dead? Mauled by a Bengali tiger? What?'

'. . . And Travis!' Frankie squeaked. 'She's at his place. She stayed over!'

'She didn't!' Marina sat bolt upright. Sure they'd talked about stuff like that. But hey – she hadn't expected it to actually happen!

'She did!' Frankie insisted. She was feeling so weird about this. What was it? Jealousy? Yeah – that was it! 'It says here on my phone – she stayed at his place. She's still there now!'

Travis fought hard to keep out the knowledge that at some point – in fact, sometime soon – he and Sinead would have to get out of bed.

Sinead reached out an arm and tweaked the edge of the naff, flowered curtain. A blade of bright sunlight flashed into the room.

'Aagh!' Travis moaned.

'I know, but it's two o'clock.'

'Two in the morning. Come back to sleep.'

'Not morning. Two o'clock in the *afternoon*.' Warmth. The touch and smell of his skin. She gave in. 'OK, I'm never going to move ever again,' she promised.

This was totally different. This feeling. Funny – it reminded him of stroking his puppy when he was eight years old. He just wanted to cuddle her and run his hand through her hair. Hey, that was seriously weird – comparing Sinead to a puppy!

'Except that I suppose we should,' Sinead sighed, resting up on her elbows.

'Did I tell you, your shoulders drive me crazy?'

'My shoulders?' She slid back under the duvet. 'They're too skinny. They've got knobbles.'

'Don't tell me – another hang-up.' He nibbled the bony bits.

'No, we have to get up!' she cried, throwing off the cover.

He pulled it back. 'Give me one good reason.'

'There's a day out there. Things to do. And the sun's shining.'

Bang! The crash of the front door told them that Rob was back from Manchester.

'Trav, you awake, mate?' Rob yelled, windswept and crumpled, clomping his big biker boots up the stairs.

'Help, I'm being stalked!' Frankie squeaked. She'd just taken a peek at the daylight and seen Lee Velcro-Boy hanging about beneath the beech trees.

'Get real, Frankie. Who would stalk you?' Marina buffed her toenails, thinking about her next move on Rob later that evening. 'We're not talking Jodie Foster . . . Madonna . . . or Gwyneth Paltrow!'

'Thanks, Marina. If you don't believe me, come and look. It's that Lee from Friday night.'

'You mean the cute one with the nice shirt?' Removing the wads of cotton wool from

151

between her toes, Marina padded over to the window.

'He's not cute. He keeps on texting me. I can't get rid of him.'

'Why would you want to?' Marina saw the solitary figure sitting on the bench. He was scuffing fallen leaves beneath his feet, hunched up, hands in his jacket pockets. 'Ah, it's dead romantic!'

'Romantic, my arse! What is there not to understand in the word, "N-O, no"?'

'Wait a sec. That's Rob coming out of Number 45.' Marina panicked and ducked out of sight as she spotted him in his leathers, carrying a helmet under one arm. She didn't want him to spot her in her trackie bottoms.

'What's he doing, Frankie? Where's he going?'

'He's fiddling with his motorbike. No, he's heading this way.' Frankie watched as Rob stopped for a couple of words with Lee. 'It looks like he knows my stalker. Right, Rob's carrying on, he's at our gate, he's coming up the path . . .'

Marina was out of there, taking the stairs two at a time. 'I haven't done my hair or anything!'

So it was Frankie who answered the door, opening it only a chink so that she couldn't be seen by Lee.

'Hi, Frankie. Is Marina in?'

She nodded and pulled him over the threshold. Then she slammed the door shut. 'Marina!' she yelled.

Upstairs, Marina messed with hairbrush and gel.

'What did that guy in the square say to you?' Frankie quizzed.

Rob shrugged.

'Did he mention me?'

'No. Why?' Rob looked up the narrow staircase as Marina made her entrance. 'Hey,' he said to her, holding out a shiny, black helmet. 'D'you wanna come for a ride?'

Marina was out on a Kawasaki and Sinead was in bed with Travis.

Frankie was alone in Number 13.

What should I do, stay or go? Frankie wondered. *Lee knows where I live. He just saw Marina go out of the front door with Rob, and I was with Marina at the club, so it's not rocket science to work out that this is my house too. Yep, he definitely knows!*

She wandered upstairs into the bathroom, sat on the edge of the bath, went back downstairs and peered through the front window. *Still there.*

`Help I'm being stalkd!` She texted Sinead, then poised with her finger over the `'send'` button. No, better not. She'd deal with this herself.

After all, Marina's parting words had been, 'Go and speak to the poor guy. Don't leave him sitting there in the cold!'

Marina, squishing her new hairstyle down under a shiny helmet. Marina, in clingy, black trousers and high-heeled boots, climbing sexily onto the pillion seat. Marina, with her arms wrapped tight around Rob's waist.

So, do I stay in and wait until he sods off, or do I go and tell him? Frankie wondered.

'I have to go!' Sinead said again.

She'd hidden under the duvet when Rob had clumped up the stairs, listened as Travis had scrambled out of bed.

'Jammy bastard,' Rob had grunted, seeing Travis in his underwear, peering into his room. 'Who've you got in there this time?'

'No one. Sod off, OK!'

Clump, clump along the landing, some cupboard doors opening and shutting, more clumping, then down the stairs and out of the house again.

And Travis had spent the next hour trying to convince Sinead that this wasn't the usual Saturday night pull and Sunday morning dalliance.

'Rob didn't seem surprised,' she'd sighed.

'What about?'

'That you had someone in bed with you.'

'It's not like that. Don't listen to him, he's a gorilla.'

'But—'

'It's not like that, Sinead. Honest.'

She'd wanted to believe him. But hey, the mood wasn't just broken, it was smashed to smithereens.

'You're not going to cry, are you?' he'd asked, trying to wrap his arms around her.

'No.' She was, but she stopped herself. *Grow*

up. It was your own decision to stay over with him.

Give Way Tonight!

Get over yourself. Get real. And she'd talked herself into kissing him again and saying everything was cool, and remembering how she'd felt when the shaft of sunlight had first hit the pillow and woken her up with Travis beside her.

But, 'I have to go,' she said now, looking for her clothes amongst his, framing the experience into an edited version she was willing to share with Frankie and Marina.

Saddo! Lee told himself. He'd texted the messages. He'd sat for an hour freezing his balls off in Walgrave Square. She must have seen him. She just didn't want to know.

You could get arrested for this, he told himself. He took one last look at the house where Frankie lived, and stood up.

'That's it, I'm out of here!' Frankie decided.

She grabbed a jacket and her borrowed camera, then dived out of the back door, down an alleyway onto the high street. She would go and take pictures of the graffiti in the underpasses, of the shop signs and traffic signals – all the urban stuff she might be able to incorporate into fresh designs for her jewellery.

She would take a bus into town.

. . . 'Hi, Frankie,' Lee said with a self-conscious grin, hanging onto an overhead strap as the bus jolted and rattled over resurfacing road-works.

'Jeez,' she breathed. 'Hi, Lee. How're you doing?'

'Good photograph.'

Tuesday morning. Frankie's eyes flashed wide as Claudia Brown stabbed her forefinger at the picture of a city-centre billboard which she'd taken on Sunday.

'You could use this section of the original image. Make an abstract design from it. Then work on it in terms of jewellery design.'

'Thanks.' Frankie nodded.

'Don't look so scared,' Claudia told her. 'I only bite students who don't take my advice!'

This last couple of days, Frankie's life had been full.

First, there'd been the conversation on the bus with Lee . . .

'Hi, Lee. How're you doing?'

'Cool. Sorry about all those texts.'

'It's OK.'

The bus had swerved and thrown Frankie against him. 'Sorry,' she'd said.

'I've been hanging about in the square.'

'I know.' *I was trying to escape, for God's sake!*

'Sorry. I'm not a perv, or anything. I'd no idea you were catching this bus.'

'I never thought you did.' She'd felt a stab of remorse.

'I just liked you, that's all.'

'Yeah, sorry.' *Look, you're not ugly or geeky or stupid or anything. Go get dancing lessons, then maybe . . .* 'This is my stop,' she'd said quickly, hopping off the bus.

Then there was Monday, in the darkroom with Travis, deliberately not talking about him and Sinead, because Sinead had got back the night before and played down the whole staying-over-at-Travis's thing and told Frankie

158

not to bother watching that space.

'Why not? I could've sworn you two were the perfect couple!' Frankie had said, keeping her own confused feelings under wraps, as usual.

Sinead had given her the Mona Lisa smile. *Don't ask. I'm not going to tell.*

So Travis had worked on Frankie's reel of photographs and she had a laugh with him over Lee being a stalker, only he really wasn't and maybe she'd been a bit hard on him, and Travis had said, yeah he knew Lee Wright. He was a final-year moving images student.

'He can't dance though,' Frankie had commented.

'I'll tell him.'

'No, don't!'

She'd got the street photos developed and printed, and brought them in on the Tuesday to Claudia's class.

'By the way, I'm pleased with your first set of designs for the ocean-based project,' Claudia said, at the end of class.

Frankie's heart leapt. Give her work over boys any day!

*

'Coffee?' Marina met Frankie in the corridor. They went to find Sinead in the sewing room.

'I've got caffeine coming out of my ears,' Sinead sighed, half an hour later, stirring her Americano. 'I'm going to try and cut down.'

'I've lost two whole pounds,' Marina claimed. 'It must be the adrenaline rush of riding pillion with Rob. How many calories do you burn off when you're scared shitless?'

Frankie and Sinead laughed. 'So, how's that going?' Sinead wanted to know.

'How's what going?'

'You and Rob?'

'Same as you and Travis,' Marina said cagily. 'Sunday on the bike was scary but cool. The gig that night wasn't my scene – lots of sweaty bodies crowded into a small space.'

'I thought that would've been *just* your type of thing,' Frankie chipped in.

'Ha-ha.' Marina turned to Sinead. 'Whenever you want to wind Frankie up, this is what you do.' Raising her hands and making a cross with her fingers, she pronounced the dreaded word, 'Lee!'

'Aagh!' Frankie cried, shrinking from the dawn like Dracula.

Wednesday. Not a good day, Marina blogged. **Sinead just had some bad news about Travis.**

'Don't tell everyone!' Frankie protested.

Am not allowed to say, she reported. **But it doesn't look good on the Sinead-Travis deal.**

Sinead was in her room, refusing to talk, but Marina and Frankie had both been there earlier that day when Suzy had delivered the killer blow.

'. . . That's what Travis does,' Suzy had been telling the girls she hung out with in the corridor after life-drawing. Jack Irvine had collared Marina to discuss her work, so Frankie and Sinead had been hanging around waiting. 'He always makes you feel special, like you're the only one, but you can never believe a guy whose sole aim in life is to get into every girl's knickers.'

'Ssh!' someone said, spotting Sinead.

Too late. Anyway, Suzy was doing it deliberately.

'I don't care who knows it,' she said. 'Travis

Quinn sleeps with everything that moves. And sometimes stuff that doesn't.'

A snigger spread like a stain down the corridor.

'Hush!' someone else said.

'So, what's new?' Suzy laughed, striding away.

It wasn't much, but it was enough. Frankie had seen the wobble in Sinead's eyes, the flicker of hurt. She'd hurried her on and out of the college, with Marina running behind, and they'd tried to hold her together.

'Suzy Atkins is a jealous cow!' Marina had insisted.

'I don't believe it. I like Travis!' Frankie had said. 'And he never tries anything on me!' *Worse luck!*

'Yeah, you're right,' Sinead had agreed, quietly. Too quietly. Then she'd refused to discuss it any more.

'It doesn't take much to shatter her confidence, does it?' Marina said to Frankie, shutting down her laptop. 'I just don't understand that about Sinead.'

'I do,' Frankie said, thoughtfully.

Marina shook her head. 'Don't tell me, it's her mother's fault. Daniella never showed her enough love or paid her enough attention when she was little, so Sinead thinks that nobody could ever love her for herself.'

'Something like that,' Frankie sighed. OK, so it sounded weak when Marina put it like that, but how come Sinead went to pieces over a nasty cow like Suzy Atkins, if it *wasn't* lack of self-worth?

'Well, I *like* Daniella,' Marina declared. 'I'd like a cool mother like her.'

'No you wouldn't.'

'Yeah I would! I'd get her to buy me a Stella McCartney dress and fly me to New York for Manolos!'

Sometimes there was no arguing with Marina.

The next day, Thursday, the For Sale sign went up outside the house.

FOURTEEN

'Hey, you can't do that!' Frankie stormed out and yelled at the guy putting up the sign.

He was bending over to nail a post to the side of the gate, his builder's bum turned towards her.

'What're you doing? Who told you to stick that there?'

For Sale. Walters and Co.

The man hammered on without replying.

'Didn't Daniella tell you?' Marina asked Sinead, standing helpless on the doorstep.

Sinead shook her head. 'I haven't heard from her since the weekend.'

'But she can't go ahead and sell this place without talking to you first!'

'Daniella can,' Sinead said, flatly. This meant

that the separation deal with Patrick was going badly.

'Take it down!' Frankie demanded. She kicked the post, but only succeeded in stubbing her toe.

The guy shrugged, packed up his hammer and left in his white pick-up truck.

'What's going on?' Frankie turned to Sinead.

'I did warn you,' Sinead said, quietly. She could feel goosebumps on her bare arms and her shoulders were hunched against the cold.

'But we never thought it would really happen!' Frankie wailed. 'We reckoned your mum would sort it, end of story.'

'Come inside,' Marina said, closing the door. 'Sinead, are you OK?'

'Yeah, fine.'

'Like Frankie said before, we'll go to the housing office and get another place, no problem.'

'Yeah.'

'But it sucks that she didn't tell us!' Frankie went on about it, until Marina glared her into silence.

'I'll ring the college,' Marina offered. 'No,

hang on, I'll call the estate agent and check there hasn't been a mistake.'

'Why can't Sinead get in touch with her mum and ask straight out?' Frankie wanted to know. Then she took a look at Sinead's pale face. 'OK, ring the agent,' she agreed.

This is meltdown! Sinead thought. *Total meltdown. My boyfriend sleeps around. My mum makes me homeless, and I'm not even worth a phone call.*

'Drink this,' Frankie insisted, coming in from the kitchen with coffee.

'When?' Marina was asking the woman on the phone. 'Yesterday. How much? Yeah, thanks.' She finished the call, then sat down beside Sinead. 'It's true,' she confirmed, not knowing what else to say.

'Bloody estate agents!' Frankie muttered, staring through the window at the evil sign.

Sinead wasn't cold any more, but she was still shaking. 'There's something else,' she told Frankie and Marina. 'If Patrick gets a big pay-off, it's not just the house that has to go.'

'What else?' Marina asked.

'Me,' Sinead told them.

'You?' Frankie didn't get it immediately.

'Yeah. If there's no money left after Patrick's taken it all, Daniella will most likely take me out of college. I'll have to go back to Dublin and live with my mother!'

'Look at that.' Rob had noticed the sign going up and called Travis to the door. 'The Gucci Girls are on the move.'

Travis hid his surprise. 'Yeah, I saw it.'

'Marina will go ballistic.'

'Stay out of her way while she's being arsy, mate.'

'I will, don't worry.' Putting on his helmet, Rob ran down the path, swung his leg over his bike and zoomed off.

For Sale. Walters and Co.

Contrary to the advice he'd given Rob, Travis's gut reaction was to go straight across the square and talk to Sinead. But something stopped him. She'd been weird with him since the weekend, and he couldn't work out why.

'Stay over,' he'd coaxed her at the start of the

week, after they'd taken in a movie together and ended up at Number 45.

'Not tonight,' she'd answered with a sad little smile. And she'd held back with the goodnight kiss.

So what had happened to their brilliant Saturday night and Sunday morning, when he'd stroked her hair and watched the sunlight dawn on her face?

And she was the same on Tuesday and Wednesday – friendly, but cagey, with shadows flitting everywhere, and things not said that should have been said and brought out into the open.

I'm confused, Travis admitted to himself, watching that blue-and-white For Sale sign. *She's inside my head, dancing around, laughing, giving me the open stare that lets me see deep down into her soul. But in real life, she's shutting down, closing me out, looking like she's hurt. What did I do?*

'Women are weird,' Rob would say. 'Don't try to understand 'em. They'll do your head in.'

'The sign stays,' Daniella told Sinead firmly,

when she'd finally plucked up the courage to call, twenty-four hours after the For Sale notice had gone up.

'I hear you. You have to sell the house.' There was no arguing with that, but Sinead felt she deserved more detail.

'It's lousy for you, darling, I know. But imagine how *I'm* feeling. I thought Patrick and I had something really special, and now he turns out to be the devil in disguise. His lawyers are jumping around, trying to screw me for every penny I've got. I realise now that I should never have put the Dublin house in joint names, but then hindsight is a fine thing. At the time, I thought we were for ever.'

Sinead didn't answer. She let Daniella talk.

'It really hurts. Honestly, Sinead, it's going to cost me a fortune in therapy and shopping to get over this one! Joke, darling.'

'I'm sorry it's worked out this way for you.'

'Well, listen, I won't go on about it. But it looks like I'm going to lose heavily on the deal that the lawyers are working out, so the Walgrave Square house will definitely have to go.'

'Right, I'll tell Marina and Frankie they'll have to move out.'

'Yes, poor darlings.'

'And, Daniella . . .' Sinead was almost choked by the question she hadn't yet asked. 'I need to know – will I be able to stay here at Central?'

'Oh.' Her mother's reaction was guarded. 'That's a hard one, honey. I haven't got the final figures yet.'

'OK, so give me a ballpark guess. What are my chances – fifty-fifty, or less?'

Daniella laughed. 'Sometimes you put things so inelegantly.'

'OK, but come on, Mum. Tell me?'

There was a long pause, then Daniella said, 'Listen, maybe I can pull a few strings with the college – talk to Tristan Fox, see if he has any influence to get you a special bursary.'

'No, don't!' Sinead pleaded. 'I couldn't bear that.'

'Mm, maybe you're right. Well, all I can tell you right now, without knowing for sure, is that you probably shouldn't put too much energy into flat-hunting for a new place with Marina and Frankie.'

*

Rob wasn't showing Marina enough sympathy for her liking.

'We're homeless!' she'd wailed, over a drink in The Alex before they moved on to a club.

'Not until the house is sold,' Rob had pointed out.

She'd told him not to argue over mere details. 'It *will* be sold though. And then what? We'll probably end up in a grotty bedsit in the worst part of town. Cracked mirrors, ancient mattresses with fleas, nowhere to hang our stuff!'

'Yeah, it's pretty hard to find decent places at this time of year,' he'd admitted.

But that had made her worse. 'Don't say that! Oh God, what are we gonna do?'

In despair, when she went to the bar for another drink, she turned to a little innocent flirting.

'Hey!' she said, recognising Frankie's Break-Dance Man. 'Lee, how're you doing?'

'Oh hi,' he said, immediately looking round for Frankie.

'She's not here,' Marina said. 'But she'll be at Strawberry Fields later.'

171

Lee's mates crowded round, eager to talk to her. She had three separate offers of drinks, and turned them all down with a lush smile and a well-rehearsed flutter of her eyelashes.

'Does Frankie think I'm weird?' Lee persevered. 'Well, yeah, I know she does. But is it terminal?'

Marina laughed. 'It's the dancing,' she advised.

His mates agreed: 'Yeah! We told you, drop the moonwalking stuff!'

From a corner of the bar, Rob watched and scowled over his empty glass. What was wrong with him? Since when did he let a woman affect his mood? But he didn't enjoy watching other guys leching over Marina, and he especially didn't like her encouraging them. *Watch it*, he told himself. *Soon you'll be telling her to button up her shirt and wear baggy trousers!*

'Here's your drink,' she said, sitting back down beside him. '"Thanks, Marina. Cheers!"' she mimicked, in the silence that followed.

He shook his head. 'I'm not in the mood.'

'Not in the mood for what? What's got into you, Rob?'

'Nothing.' *You have. Cut out the girly stuff at the bar. Let people know you're with me.*

'You can't just say "nothing",' she protested. 'There's something wrong, but you have to explain. I'm not a mind-reader, am I?'

'I don't bloody know. Who were you talking to up there at the bar?'

'Ah!' The light dawned. 'Lee Wright – you know, he's the guy who fancies Frankie.'

'And everyone else. The whole freaking football team.'

'What am I supposed to do? Wear a bag over my head and not talk?'

'Yeah, right. Fine.'

'Hey, are we having a fight?' Marina asked, eagerly seizing a chunk of leather sleeve and making Rob look up.

'I don't fight with women,' he said. He stood up, suddenly out of his depth. 'Are you coming?'

'What if I don't?' His bad mood was deeper than she'd realised. A clenching feeling in her stomach made her realise that she'd played this one wrong.

'I'm out of here,' he decided.

So she could either follow him or drift over to the bar, back to Lee and his friends, smiling as if nothing was wrong, go on to a club with a group of guys who would ogle her and dance with her, and then grab her and force her to make a quick exit – the usual stuff.

She followed Rob.

He half turned, walked a couple more steps along the pavement, then waited.

'Sorry,' Marina told him.

'I don't get it.'

'Me neither. Listen, I *never* run after a guy and say sorry!'

'I believe you. I never hang around and wait, but I just did.'

They stood under a street lamp, their gazes locked.

'You're not gonna get me talking,' he warned. 'I don't do sensitive.'

She nodded. 'Y'know what – neither do I. I do dressing up and flirty stuff. With me, what you see is what you get.'

'I like what I see,' Rob muttered.

Marina's heart jumped, missed a beat, then kick-started. 'Let's go!'

'Where?'

'I don't care. Anywhere!'

'So, are we going to the club?' Travis asked Sinead. She was stunning, her fragile face made up with dark colour around her eyes. It made them look huge, almost bruised. He wanted to hold her and say, let's not go. Let's stay here together.

'Here' was her place. Marina and Frankie were already out, but Sinead had changed her clothes a hundred times and had still been there with the bedroom light on when he'd come back to his house with a Thai takeaway. He'd decided to risk a detour and offer to share it with her.

She didn't eat. She picked like a bird.

'Yeah, let's go,' Sinead decided. She didn't know what to talk to him about, because every time she opened her mouth, stupid Suzy Atkins was on the tip of her tongue. *He always makes you feel special. But he sleeps with everything that moves.*

But the sunlight on the pillow, his eyes when he kisses you . . .

. . . And sometimes stuff that doesn't!

Sinead heard the sniggers all over again. Suzy and Co had been dissing her, making her feel small. Well, that was pretty easy to do . . .

'C'mon, let's party,' Travis said, scooping the remains of the curry into the bin and taking her out of the house, out of herself.

'Lee!' Frankie squeaked.

It was one in the morning, the club was heaving. Frankie had ended up with a couple of girls from the Jewellery course, since there was no sign of either Marina or Sinead. And now here he was, offering to buy her a drink and promising not to make her dance with him.

'Who told you?' she asked.

'Who told me what?'

'About the dancing.'

'Marina. Earlier, at the pub.'

'Huh. OK, I'll have a Bacardi Breezer. Thanks.' Whoah, she was accepting a drink from Lee – next thing she'd be agreeing to date him after all!

'You're different from other girls,' he told her.

'In a good or a bad way?'

'Good.'

'Hm, you're different too,' she replied, thoughtfully.

'Hmm.'

'No, I mean, different because I can work out what you're thinking. Most guys hide behind something – I dunno, I'm talking crap, forget it.'

'So I can relax? You won't run away again?'

'Promise not to dance?' she checked.

Lee nodded.

'Big relief,' she sighed. 'Shall we forget the drink? You can walk me home and we can talk.'

'I thought you said you didn't do sensitive,' Marina murmured.

She and Rob were stone-cold sober on a Friday night. They'd gone back to Number 45, picked up the bike helmets and ridden out of town. Now they were on top of a hill, under some trees, looking down at a twinkling carpet of city lights.

'You've changed, you're different,' he told her, between kisses.

'In what way?' It was like they were floating.

There was a world below, a dark sky above.

'Not so scary,' Rob said.

'Bad,' she frowned. 'You're supposed to be scared. Look, but don't touch!'

'Well, tough.' He kissed her again.

'Hey, Travis, hey, Sinead!' Suzy said, like she was hiding a private joke from them.

Travis nodded, then tried to squeeze him and Sinead past his ex. But it was closing time and the exit to Strawberry Fields was jammed.

'Nice skirt.' Suzy ran her eyes lazily up and down Sinead's outfit. 'Where did you get it – did Mummy buy it from a little place on Fifth Avenue?'

'No.' Thank God, they were past Suzy and heading for the fresh air, leaving the ex to stare after them and discuss Sinead with her mates.

'It's Suzy, isn't it?' Travis challenged Sinead. The penny dropped, just like that. 'You've let her come between us.'

'She's still into you,' Sinead pointed out.

'Well, I'm not into her.'

Sinead said nothing until they reached the top of the hill. 'Listen, forget what I just said. I know she isn't worth thinking about. But you know me, I agonise over what shade of eyeshadow to wear with which dress. So the gossip Suzy spreads around is my worst nightmare.'

Travis stopped dead. 'Suzy tells lies,' he said, flatly.

Sinead nodded.

'You didn't believe her, did you?'

'No!'

'You did. You let her get to you.'

'No.'

He turned away, shaking his head. His heart thudded, he felt empty and cold. 'Come on, Sinead, I'll take you home.'

Moron! she told herself. *Look what you just did!*

FIFTEEN

'So I blew it,' Sinead told Frankie and Marina.

'What d'you mean, you blew it?' Frankie dumped crockery into the dishwasher, then swept the kitchen floor. The estate agent had rung to warn them that the first prospective buyers would arrive to view the house at eleven-thirty.

'Travis knows that the stuff Suzy Atkins said got to me.'

'How did he find out?' Marina demanded. 'And don't ask me to lift a finger to get this place clean!' she warned Frankie, as an aside. 'If we leave it looking like a tip, no one will buy it, will they?'

'He knows because I told him.' Sinead sighed.

'Oh, nice one!' Marina groaned.

Frankie stopped sweeping. 'Wait! Let me guess. Travis wanted to know why you'd started backing off. You wouldn't tell him, but he pressurised you and eventually you had to admit it was the Suzy stuff.'

'Something like that,' Sinead agreed.

'Jeez, Sinead!' was Marina's response.

'I know. I let him down.'

'It showed you didn't trust him!'

'I know. Don't go on.'

'Did he lose it with you?'

'No. He went dead quiet and walked me home. He didn't say anything.'

'No kiss goodnight?' Marina persisted, the questions rapid and relentless.

'No.'

'No text message this morning?'

'No.'

'Yeah, you blew it,' Marina concluded.

'Sorry,' Frankie told Sinead, with a shake of her head. And, however she secretly felt about Travis, the 'sorry' was heartfelt. 'But he should realise that you're under a lot of pressure – this house, the money for the course, your mother, everything!'

'But you broke the most important rule in the book,' Marina pointed out.

'Which is?' Frankie demanded.

'Which is – never admit a weakness to a guy.'

Frankie finished with the chores, then made coffee. 'I agree. You let Travis see you were jealous, Sinead. Guys don't like that. It makes them feel trapped.'

'What is this, a postmortem?' Sinead scowled and took the coffee.

'We care, OK?' Frankie told her. 'We want to work this out. Now, either Travis acted the way he did last night because he was hurt that you didn't trust him . . .'

'. . . or because what Suzy said about him was true, and he *does* screw around with every girl in sight,' Marina jumped in.

'Just sock her in the jaw while you're at it, why don't you?' Frankie said in disbelief. She would have phrased it a little more gently.

Sinead frowned. 'I wasn't jealous,' she protested. 'It was just that, one moment it was like the sun was shining and the next it had gone behind a cloud. A perfect moment, then doubts. I don't do doubts. I'd rather be by myself.'

'Call it what you like, but to me, that's jealousy,' Marina insisted. 'Remember, the green-eyed monster?'

Sinead nodded. 'Well, whatever, it's wrecked me and Travis.'

'But maybe not for good,' Frankie pointed out. 'People get over this kind of stuff.'

'Not Travis,' Sinead predicted.

She recalled the look on his face, last night, standing at the top of the hill looking down the high street, as he told her in that flat, disappointed, empty voice, 'Suzy tells lies.'

The look that said she'd hurt him.

She didn't deserve him. 'I'm an idiot,' she said fiercely to herself, as the estate agent knocked at the door.

'This is the first reception room,' the agent chirped, showing a couple with two kids into the front room. 'It has an attractive bay window, an original fireplace, and feature plaster cornices.'

The kids rolled on the giant floor-cushions while their parents took in the spiel.

'The house has been rewired throughout.

New central heating system, stripped floors, and in the kitchen the present owner has installed new units, a Belfast sink and solid granite worktops.'

'They're going to buy it!' Frankie groaned, tripping over a kid.

'I can't bear it. If you need me, I'll be over at Rob's place,' Marina said, leaving without bothering with clothes, make-up or hair.

'If I were them, I'd buy it!' Frankie insisted, as the agent led the people upstairs. 'No renovation stuff to do, overlooking the square, close to town – it's like the "after" version in *Elle Deco*.'

Sinead nodded. She and Frankie waited downstairs while the viewing went on in the bedrooms.

'Does the house come with vacant possession?' the husband was asking, as they came down.

'Yes, absolutely. The girls move out as soon as contracts are exchanged.' The estate agent smiled, winningly. Frankie and Sinead scowled.

'Is this a big student area?' the wife wanted to know.

The agent answered smoothly. 'By no means. Walgrave Square is very much up and coming. And there's already been a lot of interest in this property – all of it from people looking for a family home.'

The couple nodded and smiled, while their kids dived over the back of the sofa and wrestled.

'We'll go away and talk about it,' Mr and Mrs Prospective Buyer decided at last. Nod and smile, nod and smile.

The estate agent showed them out, ignoring the girls' withering glares.

'What are we – invisible?' Frankie objected. Her watch said twelve, and she was due to meet Lee in town in half an hour. 'I mean, we're only students, not real people you have to say goodbye and thanks to!'

'Thanks, Frankie.' Out of the blue, Sinead gave her a quick hug. Her life was in limbo, but at least she knew who her friends were.

'Hey, what was that for?'

'Nothing. Just thanks, that's all.'

'Is this a date?' Lee asked.

Frankie faked a look of horror. 'This is just a Big Mac and a can of Diet Coke,' she reminded him.

'How about taking in a movie?'

'Sorry, no time. I'm going to college.'

'Not even an art-house movie later tonight?'

Frankie ditched her tray of leftovers in the bin, then nodded. 'OK. Sounds good. What time?'

'Eight o'clock. I'll meet you in the college entrance hall.' Lee leaned over and pecked Frankie on the cheek. 'Was that a kiss?' he quipped.

'No, this is a kiss,' she replied impulsively, doing it for real.

Frankie was totally into working on her piece based on the ocean. She loved the blue of the lapis lazuli, the sheen of the old gold. Sea and sand, fashioned in gemstones and precious metal.

'How do you fancy taking pictures of some new stuff for me?' she asked Travis, who was spending Saturday afternoon in his darkroom. 'It's not finished, but it would be cool to have photographs from each stage of the work.'

So he came to the jewellery workroom and worked out lighting and angles while Frankie went on polishing.

'You OK?' she asked him, without looking up.

'Yeah, why?'

'Nothing. You're quiet, that's all.'

Travis checked the focus and shutter speed. 'You want me to tell you a joke?'

'If you like.'

'Nope.'

'Didn't think you did.' Frankie moved out of shot for Travis to take the first picture. She watched him work, felt an atmosphere between them that had never been there before. 'You're sure you're OK?' she checked.

He moved round the table and took another shot. 'Why? Did Sinead say something?' *Click, click.*

'No, she didn't. Well, yes, she did. She said she'd been an idiot.'

Travis stayed silent for a long time. 'I really thought Sinead and me had something.'

It was Frankie's turn to stay quiet. Something

weird was happening, and suddenly she really didn't want to hear about how Travis felt about Sinead. In fact, it gave a jolt to her heart.

'I really rated her,' he confessed. 'I probably shouldn't be saying this to you, but I feel like I've been kicked in the guts.' *Click.*

This was where Frankie would have normally stepped in with, 'Why don't you give it another go? I'm sure Sinead does trust you, only she's dead insecure. She needs you to say how much she means to you.' But instead, she put herself first for once and said, 'Yeah, it hurts like hell, I guess.'

Click. 'I don't usually let women get to me the way Sinead did.'

'Did?' Frankie echoed. 'Is that past tense?'

Travis nodded. 'I'm over it.'

Another half-halt to Frankie's pounding heart. The first jolt was jealousy, the second temptation. *Jeez, don't even go there!* Why was she suddenly intent on moving in on Travis?

There had never been anything between her and him. They were mates, he gave her camera tips and took care of her.

Sure, she'd always known he was gorgeous,

and sure, she knew every first year on her course drooled over him. And she totally knew why Sinead had fancied him. In her head, she knew. But now, her heart and nerve-endings were feeling it too.

Travis looked up at her. 'What?'

'Nothing. Carry on.' *Click, click.*

And then there was Lee, who she'd just kissed, who she was due to meet in an hour.

This doesn't happen to me! Frankie thought. *I don't move in on my mates' boyfriends. I don't two-time.*

'Do you want a picture from this angle as well?' Travis asked. 'Or is what we've got good enough?'

'Enough, thanks.' Last *click*.

'And don't say anything to Sinead about – y'know.'

'I won't,' Frankie promised, melting inside at the view of Travis's profile, head still bent, caught in the bright white glare of the photography lamp.

SIXTEEN

'You can go off people,' Marina said.

Daniella had arrived unannounced, with her Louis Vuitton bags, her tip-tappety heels and her high-maintenance neuroses.

'I am *so* through with men!' she'd announced. 'Patrick Skinner can rot in hell for all I care. As for your bastard father, Sinead – when I asked him to top up the maintenance to pay for your college fees, he gave me a point-blank refusal!'

Frankie and Marina had cringed. That was something Sinead just didn't need to know!

'Can you believe what he said?' Daniella had gone on, ruthlessly ignoring Sinead's effort to change the subject. 'He said, why didn't I sell the house in Provence to raise some extra cash? He *actually* said that. And he knows that place is my refuge from the world. I go there every summer for the sake of my sanity. If I didn't have heavenly Provence and the lavender and the sunflowers, I'd be a total wreck!'

'You can sleep in my room,' Sinead had suggested, super-quiet now, taking her mother's bags upstairs.

'Life sucks,' Daniella had sighed, expecting lashings of sympathy and an unending supply of black coffee from Marina and Frankie.

'That woman is unbelievably selfish!' Marina pointed out, the following morning. 'A house in Provence! Sunflowers! She has all these houses everywhere, but she won't pay to keep Sinead in college!'

Daniella had hauled Sinead off to a bistro for a Sunday lunch of rocket salad.

'Yeah, but remember her world just fell apart,' Frankie pointed out. 'People are never at their best when their guy walks out on them.'

'Stop being nice!' Marina threatened. 'I don't even care that she looks like Audrey Hepburn in *Breakfast At Tiffany's*. No way should she be dumping on Sinead the way she is.'

'I agree with that,' Frankie said quietly. She picked up a text message from Lee: Thnks fr 1st nite. C u ths a m?

Guess what – Frankie has found a hunky guy! Marina blogged, with nothing better to do.

I've got one too. Sinead just lost hers.

Frankie tutted. 'Enjoy!' she sighed, texting Lee back to say she'd meet him in town in fifteen minutes.

What's happening to me? Marina blogged. **I'm Ms Untouchable, the ultimate Gucci Girl – that's what Rob calls me.**

I dress up. Marilyn is my idol and diamonds are a girl's best friend. I'm into fashion and driving guys wild.

And now look at me. I ride pillion on a Kawasaki. I get helmet-hair and sometimes I don't even care that I've forgotten my hairbrush. I kid you not. Soon there'll be grease under my fingernails and I'll be changing a spark plug! OK, maybe not. But I definitely smell of Eau de Diesel. Yuck! It's all down to

hunky Rob and his bad habits, but don't get me wrong – I'm not complaining.

Which is another major change. Normally I'm Little Miss Moaner (the Moaner Lisa, ha-ha). This isn't right, that isn't right. The guy's hair is too long/too short, his shirt is naff, he should do weights down the gym. But not Rob.

Rob *is* Marlon Brando. He's Brad Pitt and Johnny Depp rolled into one. And now I find he does do sensitive after all. That's a killer, isn't it?

Anyway, I'm looking out of the window and here comes my hero right now, crossing the square to my house (*my* house, but for how long?), carrying two bike helmets. Looks like we're going for a ride . . .

'So, who's your all-time favourite director?' Frankie asked Lee. She was struggling, big time.

'Bunŭel.'

'Favourite movie actor?'

'Garbo. What is this, speed-dating?'

She was using the questions to keep him at arm's length, too busy thinking about Travis to

193

concentrate on Lee. In fact, face it – she was using him, period.

Last night they'd taken in a movie, this morning they were walking in the park. But it wasn't working – her head was full of Travis.

'I don't think this is going to happen,' she told him out of the blue, staring mournfully at the ducks. 'I'm sorry, Lee, we'd better can it.'

He bit his lip. 'Fine,' he nodded.

'No, not fine. But I'm sorry, I'm not really into this. It wouldn't be fair. Better to stop now.'

'Yeah.' He looked down at the grass, closed his eyes, then looked up at her. 'Frankie, I really like you. I hope you have a nice life.'

'Don't be kind!' she pleaded. 'I don't deserve it. You'll find someone much better . . .'

Lee shook his head. 'So it was the dancing, huh?'

'No, not the dancing. It's me. I'm all over the place. I'm not ready for a relationship.' *I just want to make jewellery, study fashion, talk to Travis . . .*

The ducks swam up, looking for bread.

'See you around, then?' Lee said with a rising, insistent question mark.

'Yeah, at college,' she nodded.

'You won't blank me?'

'No.'

'But this is goodbye?'

'Goodbye, yeah.' Frankie turned and walked away in her jeans and big sweater, along the edge of the misty pond, towards the memorial to a dead prince, back on the main street.

By another stretch of water, way out of town, Marina and Rob sat and watched the world go by.

'Look at the ducks!' Marina pointed to two birds bobbing their heads under the surface, sticking their arses in the air. 'Sweet!'

'Why do women go ga-ga over animals?' Rob wondered.

'The same reason men hero-worship David Beckham.'

'We don't.'

'Some do.'

'No, that's just the women. They drool over his pecs.'

'How come you never agree with anything I

say?' Marina asked, snaking her arm around his waist.

'I do sometimes.'

'You bloody well don't.'

'Here we go again!' Turning in to her, he rested his forearms heavily on her shoulders. 'You're like a guy, you know that?'

'Aagh!' Marina scrambled free. 'That's the worst thing anyone has ever said to me!'

He caught her by the hand. 'I'm not kidding. You argue like a guy. You don't look like one though.'

Marina took his kiss on a slightly turned cheek, pretending to be cross.

'You don't kiss like one either.' This time he made sure that her lips met his.

Marina admitted defeat. Soon they were resting back against a rock, then slipping until they lay together in the long, dry grass.

'Aagh!' Marina said again.

'What?'

'Creepy-crawly thingy – on my neck. Get it off!'

'It's only grass seed.' Rob whisked it away with his fingertips. 'Wuss.'

'Well, it's better than being accused of being a bloke!' More kisses, soft and warm.

'Are you cold?' Rob asked, sitting her up to put his jacket around her.

'I can't believe I'm doing this!' she sighed, shoulders hunched, gazing out across the grey lake. 'How come I'm not on a yacht in the Bahamas, sipping champagne?'

'Because you're with *me*,' he grinned. 'And you love it.'

'I love *you*,' she said. *The words just slipped out, dammit.*

Rob drew back for a clearer view of her face. 'Wow,' he said, quietly.

Dammit. Tears came to her eyes.

That was the moment for Rob, when Marina's defences came down, and he saw her lip tremble and tears well up. It was moments like this that turned your life on its head, like the ducks on the lake, arses in the air.

'Yeah, me too,' he admitted.

'Life is full of surprises,' Daniella told Sinead. She was growing philosophical after a glass and a half of Merlot. 'A year ago – six months even – who would have thought that Patrick and I would split?'

'Yeah, you thought it was for ever,' Sinead consoled.

'I always do!' her mother said, with a wry laugh and a slight shake of her head. 'But I don't regret it. Who said that regrets were just lessons we haven't learned yet? Oh, it was in a song.'

'What does that mean?' Sinead wanted to know. With her mum in a softer mood, she didn't mind talking about L-I-F-E. At least it took her mind off Travis.

'Search me. But it sounds good. Regrets are lessons we haven't learned yet. So what did I learn from this one?'

'Not to sign away half your house?'

'Yeah, that.' Daniella swirled the wine around her glass. 'And not to trust another man as long as I live.'

Sinead smiled. So that was where she got her doubts from – they were inherited, pro-grammed into her genes. 'That would be a shame,' she pointed out.

'No, I plan to live an independent life from

now on,' Daniella insisted. The waiters were hovering now, obviously wanting to clear the table, but not wanting to upset a new customer. 'And what about you, darling?' she asked her daughter, suddenly overcome by a rare maternal fit. 'You look pale, you know. Gorgeous, of course, but pale.'

'And interesting?' Sinead offered.

Daniella's eyelids flickered, the corners of her mouth turned up, then she checked herself. 'Seriously, darling. Is something the matter? Have you got boyfriend trouble?'

'No way!' Sinead dropped her gaze to hide her startled expression. 'Mum, I haven't even been here for half a term yet. How could I possibly have got involved with a man?'

'You look stressed out,' Travis told Frankie, when he bumped into her as she wandered back into Walgrave Square.

Yeah, by my totally out-of-order, lustful feelings for you, which I'm doing my best to ignore! she thought. *And as luck would have it, I stumble right over you.*

'I'm OK,' she shrugged.

'College problems?' he asked.

'No, all that's great. Claudia's being nice to me.'

'Yeah, I heard.' Strolling alongside, Travis decided that Frankie needed a coffee and a chat, so he steered her towards Number 45. 'Guy problems?'

She nodded. *If only he knew.* 'Lee and I just finished.'

'Hmm.'

'Yeah, I know. We never really started. It's no big deal.'

The house was empty, looking like a bomb had hit it as usual. Rob's bike mags were scattered across the kitchen floor, greasy plates and mugs festered in the sink.

'There are plenty of guys out there for you, Frankie,' Travis reassured her. 'You're great-looking, you know that?'

Whoah! Frankie felt dizzy under his gaze. She clutched her hot mug, sipped and swallowed hard.

Travis cleared a space on the telly-room sofa and sat her down. 'The problem with you is you don't know it. I mean, most girls play on their looks, they sock you in the jaw with their legs and their cleavage. But not you. That's what's cool about you.'

'Thanks,' she gasped, deliberately scalding her tongue to keep her mind off the fact that he'd sat down next to her.

'I'm not making a play for you,' Travis explained, carefully. 'We're mates. You're feeling down. I'm trying to cheer you up, OK?'

So big brother Travis was asking her to snuggle up on the sofa, putting a friendly arm around her shoulder. God, this was agony!

Temptation. Like a little kid with a cream cake. No one will notice if you just dip your finger in and take a little lick . . . Besides, this is doing wonders for my poor old ego!

Travis picked up the vibe. His eyes narrowed slightly, his head went to one side.

'Thanks,' Frankie muttered, her skin hot and prickly beneath her furry sweater. *Get a grip!*

'For what?' Travis moved in closer, holding his breath. He was used to seeing Frankie with the girls, with a smile on her face, finding everything funny, losing stuff, confusing things, saying, 'Come on, let's go!' But now she wasn't smiling, she was gazing at him with big, serious, deep, dark eyes.

'For . . .' she faltered.

Travis leaned forward and kissed her on the lips.

They sprang apart as if they'd touched a live wire.

'Sorry!' Travis said.

'Sorry!' *Jeez, now look what you've done!*

'Forget I did that!' Travis pleaded.

Frankie stood up. 'Yeah, that was stupid,' she agreed. *But, hey, Travis and Sinead aren't together any more. Where's the harm in me taking my share of the action?*

'Now you're thinking I move in on every girl I meet, just like Suzy says,' Travis grimaced.

'No, I'm not!'

'You are. And I can see it looks that way. I'm sorry, Frankie, honest – I don't know what came over me.'

'Don't be sorry.' *I'm not.* 'It's cool. I understand.' *Time to go. Time to sort out this mess inside my head.*

'I'll see you.' Travis watched her make her getaway. *Jeez, why did I do that?*

202

'Yeah, in college,' she nodded. It was raining outside, the steps were slippy, the pavement dark and shiny.

As she closed the door behind her, Rob and Marina zoomed into the square on his gleaming machine, laughing and glowing. Frankie dug her hands deeper into her pockets, and headed out into the rain.

SEVENTEEN

'Yes, I want you to book me in for a Triple Oxygen Facial with Anita for two o'clock on Thursday,' Daniella told the girl on the phone.

Marina glanced at the glossy brochure spread out on the coffee table. 'A delicious performance that gets better and better. Don't move in case you miss something . . . an intensive treat designed to make your skin as soft and conditioned as a twelve-year-old's . . . hydrogen-peroxide creams . . . action-packed dermal makeover . . . fruit acid wash . . . hydrating enzyme pack . . .'

'Wow, it costs a hundred and thirty quid!' she gasped.

'. . . The bathroom has a low-level flush toilet,

a state of the art power-shower and is tiled throughout,' Ms Estate Agent was telling more clients.

'What do you *mean*, Patrick won't talk to me direct?' Daniella demanded, back on the phone.

Frankie hid in the kitchen but couldn't help overhearing.

'Sinead, I can't believe this!' Daniella hissed across at her daughter, one hand over the receiver. 'Patrick's dogsbody of a secretary is telling me that I can't speak to him! Now listen, Miss Rotweiler, you put that goddam son-of-a-bitch on the phone right now, or I'll fly out to New York and personally scratch your eyes out! . . . No, I will *not* contact him through his lawyers . . . No! Oh, get off my case, you jumped-up little floozie!'

Frankie sighed and left by the back door.

'. . . There's parking space round the back of the house and a permit-holders-only system on the square itself.' The estate agent continued the tour.

'Caspar, I want you to slap a writ on Patrick's so-called personal assistant for defamation of character . . . yes, I'm serious! . . . I won't be slandered by some little *Sex and the City* reject in last season's Manolos and Versace cast-offs! Have you any idea what she called me . . .?'

Sinead had reached an all-time low. Hordes of people were coming to view the house, her mother was endlessly complaining on the phone, Frankie had gone weird and quiet on her, while, worse still, Marina was blissfully happy.

'Rob and I are official,' she'd confided on Sunday night. 'It's heaven. He's the best.'

'So how come you two are still fighting all the time?' Frankie had asked. 'Every time you get together, you scrap.'

('That's not how you spell "acceleration",' Marina would say, tracing her long fingernail across the computer screen as Rob used her laptop to email a mate. 'It's got two "c"s and one "l".'

'Yes, Miss!' Rob would sulk back. 'Listen, I don't have to bloody spell it – I just do it!')

'So what?' Marina retorted. 'That's what we do. We fight. It's fun. Anyhow, what happened with you and Lee?'

Frankie shrugged. 'There *is* no Lee and me. Period.'

Through the whole of Monday and Tuesday at college, she'd been avoiding him and Travis. And to tell the truth, she'd been avoiding Sinead as well, which felt seriously bad.

'Are you OK with me?' Sinead had asked her just last night. 'Only, you seem a bit quiet.'

'Yeah, sorry. I'm really tired,' Frankie said, fobbing her off.

'Me too.' Sinead hadn't been into college all day. Marina had passed on a message from Tristan Fox that she was behind with her assignment, which hadn't made her feel any better.

So she *really* wasn't in the mood for the estate agent the following morning. She had been alone in the house until the agent had arrived with more eager buyers. Now she was in her bedroom, overhearing the usual spiel.

'. . . There's a small cloakroom leading off from the hallway.' The estate agent opened the door with a flourish. 'Also tiled throughout. We've had considerable interest already.'

'Would the vendor be open to offers?'

207

'That depends on your status as a buyer. Are you part of a chain?'

Blah-blah. Footsteps trooped up and along the landing. Sinead turned on some music to let them know she was there. *Get out of my space!*

'It seems a bit expensive to me,' the guy was saying to his partner as the estate agent opened Sinead's door without knocking.

'So, what are we going to do about Sinead?' Marina asked Frankie, after she'd sent Rob off to find a place for them to sit in the crowded coffee bar. She and Frankie were standing in the queue at the counter.

Frankie ordered coffee and a doughnut. 'Boy, I need a sugar fix!'

'Am I talking to myself here?' Marina protested, ordering two coffees, plus fries and a burger for Rob. 'Anyhow . . . about Sinead?'

'Well, we should get an exclusion order on Daniella for a start,' said Frankie. 'That woman shouldn't be allowed within two miles of the house.'

'Except that it belongs to her,' Marina

pointed out, helpfully, fighting her way through the crowd towards Rob.

'Rob, what are we gonna do about Sinead?'

'What's wrong with her? Is she sick?' Rob hadn't seen Sinead around lately.

'No, Rob, she's not sick, except in the sense of being eaten up by the green-eyed monster.'

'Jeez,' he said, through a mouthful of burger. 'What's she on about?' he asked Frankie, nodding towards Marina.

'She thinks Sinead is jealous of all the women Travis has ever slept with,' Frankie explained. Even saying the name, 'Travis', sent tiny electric shocks through her. She avoided looking up from her doughnut.

Rob frowned. 'Run that by me again?'

Marina took over. 'Sinead can't handle the fact that Travis is the best-looking guy in college – except for you, Rob, natch. OK, so he has a reputation for sleeping around, but hey, who wouldn't, when you're so drop-dead gorgeous that girls literally throw themselves at you?'

'Yeah, they do,' Rob acknowledged. 'But that doesn't mean to say Travis shags 'em all.'

'He doesn't?' Marina checked.

'No way. The guy has standards.'

Frankie licked the sugar from her lips. She so didn't want to be listening to this!

'Personally, if I were Sinead, I'd see it as a challenge,' Marina went on. 'I'd just go ahead and prove to everyone that I could hang onto the world's most shaggable guy.'

'Got it,' he muttered. 'But Sinead can't take the heat?'

'No, because the lovely Suzy over there spread the wicked word while Sinead was standing right next to her.' Marina didn't look over her shoulder, but she knew Suzy Atkins was huddled around a nearby table with her mates. 'Sinead went to pieces and has hardly spoken to Travis since.'

'Women!' Rob spat, mid-munch.

'Watch what you say,' Marina warned. 'We outnumber you, we're cleverer than you, and we also have a higher pain threshold . . .'

'Yeah, yeah, whatever.'

'Rob, you couldn't talk to Travis about this, could you?' Marina suggested after a while. 'Y'know, help get Sinead and Travis back together as a couple? They're so right together – everyone can see that . . . well, apart from Sinead, but she's got a lot on her mind with all these problems with the house and Daniella.'

'No.' Rob said point-blank.

'No, I agree,' Frankie added, for less than straightforward reasons.

Marina sniffed. 'OK, so give me a better idea.'

'Let me think about it,' Rob said, scraping back his chair and heading off to his work-shop.

'*What?*' Frankie frowned. She knew Marina was staring at her, even though she couldn't meet her gaze.

'What's with you?' Marina demanded. 'How come you're so low on ideas all of a sudden? Don't you *want* Sinead and Travis to get back together?'

'*Ssh!*' Frankie warned, feeling her cheeks flush bright-red as Travis walked in to order a coffee.

'You really are coming on in leaps and bounds,' Jack Irvine told Marina. He studied her portrait sketch of the middle-aged model. 'This face is anatomically correct, plus your drawing conveys a real atmosphere. It's bold and uncompromising. Nice work.'

To Marina, the sitter looked as though she'd been through life's mill and come out a bit crushed. There were folds in her skin, frown lines between her eyes, and her upper lids were drooping. She looked sad and weary. Yet she was probably about the same age as Daniella.

No Triple Oxygen Facials there, then, Marina thought, glancing across at Frankie's sketch.

Frankie had made the woman blue. Early Picasso. All angles, and the eyes at odd levels.

'Interesting,' Jack said, in passing. 'Where's your friend, what's her name, the tall one with cropped, blonde hair?'

Frankie shook her head, then shrugged.

'Pah, another one bites the dust,' the gritty life-drawing tutor grunted. 'They drop like flies during this first term, believe me.'

Marina stood back to study her portrait. *So how much Botox has Daniella had?* she wondered. *And what other nips and tucks? And would she, Marina, resort to plastic surgery when she reached thirty? Probably. Why not? Then again, it most likely hurt like hell.*

'Thanks, Jo!' Jack called, as the class ended and the ground-down woman scooped up her dressing-gown from the floor.

'Guess what Rob told me last night,' Marina said to Frankie, amidst the packing up of charcoals and pastels.

'About what?' Frankie hadn't slept much since Sunday. She'd seen Travis once, in the jewellery workshop, and stumbled through a stilted conversation with him. He'd felt as bad as her, obviously.

'About Suzy Atkins.'

Rob had come up with a little nugget of information – just tossed it into conversation, saying it might help the Travis-Sinead situation. She'd thrown her arms around him and kissed him gratefully. 'You're a star, Rob Evans! A lowdown, cunning, sneaky star!'

'It'll have to wait,' Frankie said after life-drawing, hastily making her exit. 'I've got a one-on-one tutorial with Claudia. Sorry, Marina, I've got to go!'

'Ten *thousand* pounds!' Daniella was acting as though the estate agent had just admitted to being a serial killer and a terrorist all rolled into one. 'Tell me you're joking. You're saying their offer is ten grand short of the asking price?'

'They're cash buyers,' the agent reminded her, eyeing Daniella nervously. Then he glanced sideways at Sinead, standing quietly beside her mother.

Daniella had insisted on dragging Sinead out of the house for some retail therapy. ('You're looking so dowdy, darling. Let's shop for some new tops, and perhaps get Jade to take a glance at your hair.') By chance they'd passed Walters and Co and called into the office.

'And it's our only firm offer,' the suit behind the desk said. 'I took the call from Mr and Mrs Yates half an hour ago. I've been trying to get in touch with you to put their figure to you.'

'Ten grand!' Daniella sighed. 'God, I hate selling houses. It's enough to sour your view of humanity for good!'

Sinead went to look at the board of houses for sale. So this was it – there was an offer on Number 13. The end was in sight for her short and far-from-brilliant career at Central College. Like a firework that never went off, her dreams of glitz and sparkle, of exploding onto the fashion scene and eclipsing all rivals, fizzled out.

'Tell Mr and Mrs What's-their-name to meet me halfway,' Daniella spat out. 'Five grand below the asking price, and not a penny less!'

OK, so she could do this without Frankie, Marina decided. This couldn't wait. It needed to happen now.

Finding Suzy Atkins in the second-year hang-out zone wasn't difficult. Marina made straight for the corner of the top-floor cutting room where she knew Suzy would be – and yeah, there she was, surrounded by hangers-on, perched cross-legged on a stool, fiddling with a pair of cutting shears, *snip-snipping* her way through people's lives like the lousy gossip-monger she was.

'Yeah?' Suzy challenged, as first-year Marina plunged into the midst of their conversation.

'Stewart Brown.' Marina dropped the two words in and waited.

Suzy slammed the scissors onto the table. A few hangers-on fell away, sloping off to their own tables or in search of an imaginary missing needle and thread.

'What about him?' Suzy growled.

'Stewart Brown, last Friday night, Strawberry Fields,' Marina said slowly.

'So?'

Marina realised that this was one startled chicken, about to squawk. *Thank you, Rob!*

'First, he's way too old for you,' she pointed out.

'I didn't . . . we never . . . get lost!' Suzy stammered.

'Second, he's married.' Marina was enjoying this moment, savouring it even.

Suzy's mouth screwed up into a tight purse. 'Who's been telling you this stuff?'

'Never mind.' In with the killer blow, eyeball to eyeball. '. . . Married to Claudia,' Marina said. 'Y'know – Claudia Brown, Head of

Jewellery here at the college? And, I believe, your personal tutor!'

'I did it, I told her!' Marina laughed with Frankie, on the way home to Walgrave Square. The rush-hour streets were dark, the shop windows already gearing up for Christmas with glittery party dresses and cheesy Santa sleighs. 'You should have seen her face! And none of her so-called mates stuck up for her! No – they just watched her squirm.'

'So now what? Has she agreed to talk to Sinead?' Frankie fought hard to get her head around the facts. It seemed it came down to blackmail.

'Too right she did!' Marina said. 'Imagine what would happen if Claudia ever found out that her husband had been fooling around in a club with one of her students? Exit one husband *and* one student!

'But I'll say this for Suzy – she's not stupid. She got the picture. When I said all she had to do for me to keep quiet was to come and talk to Sinead and tell her she'd been lying about Travis, well . . . she nearly bit my hand off!'

'She agreed,' Frankie said flatly. *Make like you're glad for Sinead!* she told herself.

'Exactly. And anyway, according to Rob, this image that Travis has is total garbage. He's much too nice a guy to jump into bed with every woman who comes on to him. In fact, he's really shy with women. Can you believe it?'

'Yeah,' Frankie sighed. 'Much too nice.' *And don't I know it!*

'So everything's going to be hunky-dory between him and Sinead!' Marina was fizzing with excitement. 'Frankie, I feel like a fairy godmother, I totally do!'

Then they turned the corner onto the square. There was a pick-up truck outside Number 13, and a fresh notice was being fixed across the For Sale sign.

'Hey!' Frankie protested, running two or three steps, then stopping under the trees in despair.

'Oh, no!' Marina groaned.

The guy stepped back from the sign, flung his hammer into the truck, then climbed in and drove off.

'Sold', the notice read. Marina and Frankie read it twice, then three times: 'Sold, Subject to Contract.'

EIGHTEEN

Get a grip! Sinead told herself. *The house is sold and Travis is history.*

With these facts in mind, she chose her outfit for one last Friday night on the town. Whatever happened, she was going to go out in style.

She picked out a low-cut, silver sequin top with asymmetric, grey chiffon sleeves; pulled on a pair of slinky, silver hotpants; teamed them with her black-and-grey Louis Vuitton platforms, then spiked up her ash-blonde hair.

'I thought you'd be crushed,' Frankie said, encountering rock-chick Sinead on the stairs. She and Marina had rushed into the house, ready with the hugs and sympathy. 'What happened?'

'I'm going out with a bang,' Sinead

explained. 'If you've gotta go, make sure you make a big exit.'

'Right!' Marina agreed, racing off to find her glammest frock.

'Where's Daniella?' Frankie asked in a worried voice, failing to take in Sinead's personality transplant.

'Gone.'

'Gone where?'

'Dublin. Now that this place is sold, she can finalise her deal with Patrick.'

'But what about you and college?'

The new brash and bold Sinead faltered over this one. Then, bravely: 'I'm kissing goodbye to Miu Miu and Missoni. Au revoir, Alexander McQueen!'

'Oh, honey!' Marina sighed, sticking her head out of her bedroom door. 'Are you sure?'

'Yeah, I'm not getting up any false hopes in that department,' Sinead said, with an empty laugh. 'But don't get me wrong – now that I know where I stand, I can cope. It was the not knowing, the doubting, that I couldn't handle.'

Frankie got it at last. 'You're cool,' she acknowledged, admiring Sinead's nerve.

'And you *look* fabulous!' Marina added, vanishing back into her room for the final transformation.

'Sold,' Travis said, staring across the square at Number 13.

'Yeah, it sucks,' Rob agreed, fuelling up with a takeaway curry, ready for a heavy night out.

'Did you and Marina talk about it?' Travis mumbled. Mumbling was meant to show he wasn't really interested in Rob's reply. And he bodyswerved the main question, which was, 'How's Sinead taking it?'

'Yeah, man. I said now that she was homeless, she could come and live here instead.'

Travis took a sharp breath. *What!*

'Only kidding,' Rob laughed. 'Those Gucci Girls, they stick together. Marina's already looking for a new place with Frankie.'

'And Sinead?' Travis mumbled.

Rob looked up from his curry. 'From what I hear, mate, Sinead has to go back to Dublin's fair city.'

'Huh.'

'Sorry.'

Travis shrugged. 'I'm over it, mate.'

'Good. Nice one.'

'I am, I mean it. Sinead's got problems. She needs to sort them out.'

This time, Rob said nothing.

'It's the trust thing. She doesn't have it.'

Silence again.

'So anyway, I have to work tonight, taking pictures at the Third-Year Fashion Show.'

'Me too, as it happens – I'm doing the music for the show. But when we finish, we can head off to the clubs.'

But Travis wasn't listening. *I'm over Sinead,* he told himself. *So over her.*

'This or this?' Marina waved a lemon chiffon confection and a peachy-cream satin number in front of Sinead's face.

'The satin,' Sinead told her. 'With your pink Fendi-style sandals with the transparent heel.'

'The ones Frankie gave me? Thanks.' Marina rushed off to squeeze her curves into the tight bodice.

'Is this OTT?' Frankie asked, appearing in a bright-green, stretch jersey mini-dress with a ruched front, big black belt, black tights with a slashed pattern woven into them, and three-inch, T-bar shoes.

'Yep,' Sinead said. She hadn't sat down for an hour in case her slinky pants creased.

'Good, I'll wear it!' Frankie grinned. 'Hair up or down?'

'Are you seeing Marina tonight?' Travis asked Rob, while he shaved.

'Later. Why?' Rob was stacking his music gear in the hallway, ready to call a cab to take him to the college.

'You two can't get enough of one another. Must be love!' Travis kidded.

Rob laughed and punched numbers into his phone. 'D'you know what?' he said. 'I think it is.'

'Ready?' Sinead asked Frankie and Marina.

'Let me put on my lippy!' Marina begged.

'Are you sure about my hair being up?' Frankie checked.

'Let's *go*!' Sinead insisted. This was it – the final curtain. '*I did it my way!*' she sang, doing a

Marina, as she opened the front door and stood, *da-dah*, on the top step.

'Where are we going?' Marina asked, curvy and sleek, glossed and glammed up, as in the pre-Rob days.

'College,' Sinead told her and dayglo-Frankie. 'It's the Third-Year Fashion Show. We're going to strut our stuff!'

Lights, music, cameras, action!
Skinny models in hotpants, camisoles and shades, sauntered out onto the catwalk. The theme of this year's show was 'Beachside'.

'It's bloody winter!' Rob had pointed out, before digging out a Beach Boys compilation. Now the sound of 'Good Vibrations' soared over their heads.

'*Good-good-good-good vibrations!*' Frankie, Sinead and Marina stood at the back of the audience, jiggling along to Rob's retro music.

A girl shimmied down the catwalk in a straw stetson and a pale-lilac ruffle dress, teamed with slouchy, tan leather boots. *Yee-hah!*

Click! Travis captured the moment on film.

A parade of white and turquoise, silver and

tourmaline, strappy sandals and fancy flip-flops followed. *Click-click-click.*

'Gorgeous!' Marina sighed, then suddenly dived forward into the rows of seats where the audience of students, tutors and proud parents sat.

Sinead and Frankie were too busy looking at Travis photographing the babes on stage to notice. The Beach Boys were singing about excitations.

'*Now!*' Marina hissed at Suzy Atkins.

'Later!' Suzy squirmed.

Claudia and Tristan were sitting directly in front of her. Claudia turned round and tutted.

'*Now!*' Marina insisted, dragging Suzy from her seat. 'Sinead's back here with Frankie. You have to tell it exactly like it is.'

'Look . . .' Suzy began, beach music from the Sixties thudding faintly in the background.

Marina, Frankie and Sinead faced her across a rack of half-made dresses, squashed between tailors' dummies in a workroom off the main hall.

'Let me out of here!' Sinead protested.

But Marina and Frankie made her stay. 'Listen!' Marina ordered.

'Look, this is stupid,' Suzy stammered.

'Tell her!' Marina insisted.

'OK, OK. What I said about Travis . . . it wasn't true.' Suzy fessed up.

Sinead stepped back and collided with a dummy, which toppled sideways into a rack of clothes.

'More,' Marina ordered.

'He doesn't sleep around.' Suzy's face was screwed up in a tight knot, as if she was in pain. 'Travis isn't the type. In fact, if you must know, we went out for six weeks and never even slept together!'

'Hah!' Frankie said.

'I just said it to get up your nose,' Suzy told Sinead. She turned to Marina. 'Can I go now?'

But Marina made her wait. 'Did you hear all that?' she checked with Sinead. 'Did you get it into your head?'

Sinead nodded. 'What did I ever do to you?' she asked Suzy.

'Nothing. Zero. Zilch. But I could see Travis was serious about you.'

'So, you were jealous,' Frankie realised. 'The most beautiful fresher in college had nicked your ex. Miaow!'

Suzy nodded. 'Can I go now?' she repeated.

The show was over and the catwalk was being dismantled. In the changing room, girls in bikinis shivered as they dug out their day clothes.

'Drink?' Rob suggested to Travis out front, as he stacked his gear into a cupboard.

'Yeah, just give me a minute,' Travis answered. 'I want to take these films up to my darkroom.'

'Sinead, wait, there's something I need to tell you,' Frankie said.

Suzy had exited minus her dignity, and Marina had shot off to bring Rob up to speed.

'What is this – Confessions Anonymous?' Sinead tried to make a joke of it, but the news from Suzy had rocked her back on her heels. Could it really be true that Travis didn't sleep around?

'No, really, it's something that's been

bugging me all week. It's all my fault – I should never have done it.'

'Why would Suzy admit that?' Sinead wondered, still fixed on the big revelation. 'What did Marina *do*?'

'Listen, Sinead . . .' Frankie felt she would break under the burden of the secret kiss. She'd fought through the jealousy and the longing, and come to her senses at last.

'Hey!' Marina burst back in on them. Another dummy toppled. 'Sinead, Travis is up in his darkroom. Go get him, girl!'

He won't want to know, Sinead convinced herself as she took the lift. *He'll just think I'm a shallow, spoilt, jealous bitch.*

The lift eased sluggishly up to the fifth floor. A *ping* told her she'd finally arrived.

I can't do this! she faltered. No, that was the old Sinead – the one plagued by doubts and insecurities. Get a grip. *I'm leaving anyway. The least I can do is tell Travis I'm sorry.*

She stepped out into the dimly-lit, empty corridor. Catching her reflection in the shiny, steel doors of the lift, she shook herself and set her jaw at an upwards tilt. Travis's room was third on the left, the one with the dim green light filtering under the door.

Tell him I'm sorry and that what we had was perfect until I threw it all away. Sinead rehearsed it in her head, took a deep breath, then knocked and went in.

Travis had his back to the door. He was stacking rolls of film into small compartments on a shelf and carefully labelling them. When he heard the door open, he turned around, expecting to see Rob.

Sinead stood uncertainly in the doorway, dressed like a medieval knight, with a helmet of pale-blonde hair and a chainmail shirt of shimmering sequins.

'Hey,' she said.

'You're leaving?' he asked.

She nodded. 'Daniella. Money. Y'know.'

'That's a waste of talent.'

'Thanks.'

'What'll you do next?'

'Live at home in Dublin, maybe try to enrol in the local college.'

Travis nodded.

'I came to say sorry.' Sinead forced back the tears. Look what she'd done – what she'd thrown away.

Travis dropped the casual act and took a step towards her. 'I know. Just one little tiny seed of doubt – it's a killer.'

'You know?'

'Yeah, it happened to me once. I thought a girl at school was two-timing me. She wasn't, but I'd already dumped her when I found out.'

'Bummer.' Sinead breathed out softly. 'Anyway, I'm sorry – I really am.' *Because what we had was perfect.*

'Yeah, it was pretty good while it lasted.' Travis tried for a throwaway style, but his heart thumped harshly in his chest. Sinead was leaving . . .

'Perfect,' she sighed, their gazes locked.

'As good as that?' he murmured.

She nodded.

'Yeah, it was.' He moved in close.

Sinead kissed him. 'I'm so, so sorry,' she said.

He kissed her lips and face. 'Stay with me. Let's try again.'

'I love you, Travis.'

'But?' he asked, standing back so that her face came into focus. 'I can hear a "but" in there, can't I?'

'But I have to leave,' she reminded him. 'I have no money of my own. I rely on Daniella for a roof over my head, and that means Dublin.'

NINETEEN

'Phone!' Marina called from the depths of the duvet. No way was she going to move a muscle to answer it.

'Ugh,' Rob groaned. 'What time is it?'

Marina squinted at her watch. 'Ten-thirty.'

'Mmm,' Rob said, snuggling in closer.

'Ergh!' The phone seemed to be ringing right into Travis's ear. 'Sod off, I'm asleep.'

'Shouldn't you answer it?' Sinead murmured, her arms locked around his waist.

'No way.'

'It's half-ten, you know.'

'Too early. I'm asleep.'

*

Brrring-brrring. 'Answer the freaking phone, why don't you!' Frankie swore into the mouthpiece.

She looked out across the dismal square at the drawn curtains of Number 45. Travis and Sinead. Rob and Marina. OK, she was going to have to take extreme measures.

Slamming down the phone, Frankie threw a manky parka over her pyjamas, slipped her bare feet into Marina's pink polka-dot mules and stormed out across the square.

'Oh God, no!' Marina groaned. 'Now someone's at the door.'

'Freaking postman,' Rob muttered, slothfully.

'Don't answer it,' Sinead pleaded, welded to Travis.

'No way. I'm going to stay here for ever with you,' he promised.

Frankie stood back from the house to glare up at the bedroom windows.

'Sinead!' she yelled, picking up a pebble from the path and chucking it.

A boy delivering papers on a bike cycled by and sniggered at her outfit.

'Sinead, I'm catching my death out here! Get out of bed and talk to me, for Chrissake!'

Sinead heard the rattle of the stone on the windowpane and sat bolt upright. Grabbing the duvet to wrap around her like the pastry on a sausage-roll, she hobbled to the window and flung it open. 'Frankie!'

'Yeah, it's me.'

Sinead stared at the bedraggled figure on the pavement. 'What happened? Did someone die?'

'No, I got a message from the estate agent. You have to come home, quick!'

'Why? What's the big deal?' Behind her, an exposed Travis struggled bashfully into his clothes.

Frankie spread her arms wide. 'It's the Yateses – the couple who bought the house.'

'What about them?'

'They're on their way over to measure for curtains!'

'Whatever!' Sinead had sighed.

But by then, Travis was dressed and conscience got the better of her. She dressed too and met a bleary-eyed Marina across the kitchen table.

Marina saw Sinead and reacted like a bomb had dropped.

'Don't ask!' Sinead warned her housemate.

Marina asked anyway. 'Sinead, what in the name of sweet Jesus are you doing here?'

'Same as you,' Sinead threw back at her.

'You and Travis . . . You said he was history . . . But . . . hey, this is cool!'

'Girls, girls!' Rob cut in, on hand with tea and toast. 'Yeah, I'm fully house-trained,' he grinned at Sinead, as she looked at him in disbelief.

'I told Frankie that we'd be at the house by eleven,' Sinead relayed to Marina, as she spooned marmalade onto a thick wedge of toast. 'Mr and Mrs Yates told her eleven-fifteen.'

'What's with the "*we*"?' Marina protested. 'How many fashion design students does it take to measure curtains?'

'I don't know, how many fashion design

students *does* it take to measure curtains?' Travis entered the kitchen, as if expecting a witty punchline.

Marina threw a chunk of sticky toast at him, which he caught and ate. 'This is no joke,' she told him, wagging a finger. 'The Yateses are ruining my beauty sleep!'

'They're the people buying the house, right?' Rob checked. A nod from Marina. He went off into a corner and began texting.

'Who are you texting?' Marina asked, her eyes smudged with last night's mascara, her hair more haystack than Hollywood.

'Some mates,' Rob grunted, whipping the phone away before she could read the message.

'Oooh, Mr Mystery!' Marina teased. Then she turned to Sinead. 'C'mon – if we're gonna do this curtain measuring stuff, let's go,' she sighed. 'Otherwise I might just lose the will to live!'

'Say we bought fabric at twenty pounds a metre,' Mrs Yates said to her husband. 'This bay window would need at least twenty-five metres, plus lining fabric, so you can reckon on at least seven or eight hundred pounds, just for this one window.'

Mr Yates squeaked like a mouse in a trap. 'What's wrong with the ones already up?'

'Jason!' Mrs Y sighed, glancing at Sinead, Frankie and Marina for sympathy over the smallness of men's brains.

Marina yawned. Frankie scratched her neck. Sinead couldn't banish visions of last night and Travis's soft breath on her cheek as she lay for the second time on his pillow.

'Actually, we forgot to ask – does the price we agreed on include carpets and curtains?' the husband asked Sinead.

'I guess,' Sinead said, with an absent-minded nod.

'This is terrible!' Frankie whispered miserably to Marina, as the buyers went from room to room with their tape measure. 'We're practically homeless. Let's face it – the Gucci Girls have hit rock bottom!'

Vroom-vroom-vroom!

'That's three-point-seven metres by one-point-five metres,' Mrs Y called out, over the roar of engines in the square.

Vroooom! A dozen gleaming motorbikes entered in a posse from a northerly direction.

'One-point-five or one-point-nine?' Mr Y yelled back.

The machines approached in formation, like the Red Arrows at fly-past. *Vrooooom!*

'What the . . .?' Mr Y protested.

Marina, Sinead and Frankie leaned out of a bedroom window. In an instant Marina recognised Rob's silver Kawasaki at the front of the leather-clad gang. Exhaust fumes filled the air. 'Oh no, not again!' she said, reacting quick as a flash.

'Huh?' Frankie muttered.

'*Sssshhh!*' Marina warned. 'Here come those Hell's Angels!' She tuned her voice to copy Daniella's best nasal tone of disapproval. '*Every* Sunday morning they congregate here. I don't know why the police don't act to ban them – all the neighbours have phoned them often enough!'

'Huh?' Frankie frowned.

Vrooooom! Twelve 1000cc engines roared in the Sunday silence.

'*And* every single evening during the week!' Marina laid it on thick. 'Don't ask me why they choose to meet here in Walgrave Square. You'd think there'd be plenty of other places for bikers to hang out!'

'For heaven's sake!' Mrs Y wailed, putting her hands over her ears.

Playing the role of a lifetime, Marina sighed and shook her head. 'Don't worry – you learn to live with it in time!'

'Yeah, live and let live,' Sinead added, after Marina had dug her in the ribs. Ah, at last, she got it!

'I recommend earplugs,' Frankie told the Yateses, catching on too. 'You'll find it helps when the bikers come round at night.'

Mr Yates pressed the button on his extendable, metal tape measure. The girls watched it shoot back into its green plastic casing. 'Come on, we're out of here,' he said to his wife.

'Horrendous!' Mrs Y bleated. 'This is exactly the sort of thing that estate agents deliberately miss out of their details.' She took one last look at the gang of thugs in the street below. 'What a terrible racket. Total hell on earth!'

*

'What happened?' Sinead asked the estate agent ingenuously, when she rang at tea-time that day.

The workman had come and altered the sign again. He'd taken away the Sold strip and exposed the For Sale sign beneath once more.

'The Yateses withdrew their offer,' the agent explained, sniffily. 'Don't ask me why. Anyway, you'd better tell your mother that the house is back on the market.'

'*Yessss!*' Frankie punched the air. Result! At least this gave them some breathing-space.

Meanwhile, Marina gave Rob a long, grateful kiss. 'Sometimes you're a genius, Rob Evans, and I love you!' she cooed.

Sinead told the agent that she would do her dirty work for her, then put down the phone. 'Daniella isn't going to be happy,' she warned the others.

'But I am,' Travis told her, taking her in his arms, while Frankie bustled off into the kitchen and noisily opened a celebratory bottle of plonk. 'It means that for as long as the house is up for sale, I get to keep you!'

241

TWENTY

Marina to the world – this is Marina calling!

'Blogging again,' Frankie grumbled. 'It's an addiction with her,' she told Travis and Rob.

It was Sunday afternoon. They were all round at Number 13. The guys were watching footie, while the girls took it in turns to stand lookout for possible house-buyers.

'I reckon the Hell's Angel trick will work as many times as we want it to,' Sinead said. 'That and the fact that Daniella is asking way too much money.'

'The longer the better,' they all agreed.

We're still in Walgrave Square, Marina typed. **Saw the Third-Year Fashion Show on Friday – beach babes galore. Have decided to**

raid the archives of the nineteen-thirties fashion houses for my next project. Balenciaga, Coco Chanel. Am gonna design a line of autumnwear based on couture collections. Wowee!

'Tell them the college is taking us to Paris in spring,' Frankie chipped in.

College is organising a trip to the spring fashion shows in Paris, Marina typed obediently.

'Yeah, and guess who won't be there,' Sinead groaned.

'That was definitely a foul!' Rob yelled. 'Did you see the way that Italian fullback went in for the tackle?'

Sinead says, guess who won't be there, Marina blogged. Then she came to a world-shaking decision. So, people – this is my last entry, she typed. OK, I know I'm leaving on a cliffhanger – will Sinead stay or will she go? – and you may never know the answer, but the fact is, I have better things to do with my time right now.

'Free kick, ref!' Rob roared, hammering the Ikea coffee table with his fist.

Like be with my wonderful, gorgeous,

243

talented, generous, clever boyfriend . . .

'Yuck!' Frankie read the last sentence in passing. She made sick noises and walked off.

Frankie says yuck, Marina blogged. **But this is goodbye to all of you out there. I have to paint my toenails and wash my hair. In any case, who needs the worldwide web when you're in love!!!!**

'You don't have to pack yet, do you?' Travis said to Sinead. They were up in her room, he was watching her take clothes out of the wardrobe and fold them carefully before she put them in a case.

'Technically, no,' she agreed. 'But this is me trying to face facts. No more college, no more Walgrave Square.'

'What about us?' he asked.

She shook her head. 'I just don't know, Travis.' Here it came again – the not knowing thing – throwing her off-balance, making her take a step backwards from the man she loved.

This time, he read the signals. 'It's weird, this kind of limbo.'

'Yeah.'

'Put that down.'

She dropped the jacket onto the bed.

He folded his arms around her and rested her head on his shoulder. 'Oh babe, I wish it would all go away.'

'You didn't!' Marina hissed.

'I did,' Frankie admitted.

Sinead and Travis were upstairs. Rob had gone out to buy a newspaper.

'You kissed *Travis*?'

Frankie nodded. 'I know – I should just find a quiet corner and shoot myself.'

'*When*?' Marina demanded.

'*Sshh!* Last week. Sinead was acting like she didn't want to know Travis, and I'd just dumped Lee. Travis was being really nice to me. I bumped into him in the square and he asked me in for a coffee. I was flattered, I admit, and I . . . oh, don't ask me what I was doing, I dunno!'

'I can't believe you, Frankie – after the way you laid into me when I *accidentally* snogged Travis at our party!' For once, Marina was lost for words.

'The thing is, I've been feeling lousy about it all week. I mean, I moved in on my best mate's bloke. That's not me – I don't do that!'

'You just did,' Marina said quietly. 'But Sinead doesn't know?'

Frankie shook her head. 'I almost told her the other day . . .'

'Wrong!' Marina cut in. 'Like, so wrong!'

'What? You mean don't tell her?' Frankie frowned. 'But I feel lousy.'

'So go ahead and tell Sinead that you got off with him, and make yourself feel better!' Marina scoffed. She could see Rob parking his bike at the gate. 'Great idea – *not!*'

'Right,' Frankie said, slowly. 'Not good, huh?'

'You tell her so *you* feel better, but then Sinead feels suicidal instead.'

'So keep quiet?'

'Too right!' Marina heard the front door open. 'Never tell a single soul – got it?'

'*Zip!*' Frankie said, sealing her lips. 'Not a word.'

And, suddenly, strangely, though she was deceiving her mate, she felt better.

*

246

'*Some enchanted evening!*' Marina sang.

The fag end of Sunday afternoon had drifted into evening, and a drink at The Alex.

'Keep it down, Marina!' Frankie begged. God, the girl was a major embarrassment when she was in love.

'*You may see a stranger. You may see a stranger, a-cross a crowd-ed room . . .*'

Rob and Travis were playing pool on the far side of the room. Marina, Frankie and Sinead hugged a radiator for warmth.

'Travis is being so nice to me,' Sinead confessed. 'He says he'll come to Dublin to see me as often as he can.'

'Nice one,' Frankie murmured. Marina flicked a glance her way.

'But *we* don't want you to go!' Marina protested. 'We're like the Three Musketeers – Arthos, Porthos and Thingummy!'

'Yeah, Central College is where you belong.' Dipping into her bag for her phone, Frankie found that it wasn't hers that was going off. 'Must be yours,' she told Sinead.

'*Some enchanted evening . . .!*' Marina hummed.

1 message received Sinead read. She pressed 'read'. Daniella, it said on the screen. Sinead pressed again. Ptrck cavd in.

Sinead dropped the phone flat on the table. Marina and Frankie craned over to read the message.

'What does she mean, Patrick caved in?' Frankie asked.

'Call her!' Marina said, eagerly.

With fingers too shaky to press the right keys first time, Sinead called her mother.

'Oh darling, good news!' Daniella began. 'But listen, I'm busy. Could you call me back in an hour?'

'No!' Sinead said firmly, her new self kicking in. 'Tell me now. I need to know.'

'OK, OK, but it'll have to be quick. My wonderful lawyer was cleverer than Patrick's cheapskate New York attorney. He boxed them into a corner and made Patrick withdraw all claims to the Dublin house.'

'When?' Sinead gasped.

'Yesterday, was it? Or Friday? Anyway, there was a lot of stuff about me being able to claim half of Patrick's investments in the stock market, which made them take a rethink on Dublin. And there you are, we have a deal!'

'Wow!' Sinead's hand shook.

'Are you still there? Must go, darling.'

'Mum – what about Walgrave Square?'

'What about it? Oh, don't worry, I'll call the agent and take it off the market.'

'And what about college?' Sinead felt the tight band around her chest slowly loosening its hold.

'Stay, darling, stay! Become a fashion designer if that's what you really want.'

'It is,' Sinead told her earnestly. To be the next Moschino or Phoebe Philo, to be up there with Ungaro and Jimmy Choo – that's all she'd ever wanted.

It was Frankie who delivered the good news to Travis and Rob.

Pow! Rob pocketed the black ball.

'Sinead can stay!' Frankie cried.

'You're kidding!' Travis said, as Sinead arrived and fell into his arms. Frankie smiled, and Marina gave her a hug.

Together, they left The Alex and ran up the hill to Walgrave Square.

Travis grabbed the For Sale sign and dragged it out of the ground. He flung it into the bin by the bare beech hedge.

'Sinead can stay!' Marina yelled to the empty square.

'Yesss!' the others cried, punching the air.

Sinead ran to the top step and spread her arms wide. 'I can stay!' she echoed, happily.

'Cool!' Marina and Frankie sighed, as they joined Sinead, put their arms around her shoulders, then sat on the doorstep and cried for joy.

The black trees dripped raindrops, lights glimmered from between half-closed curtains. Finally all five of them went into the house.

Soon music floated out onto the square. Another night, another house party. *Their* house party.

ARMANI ANGELS BY JASMIN OLIVER

Frankie, Marina and Sinead have the end-of-term, mid-winter blues. There are fashion assignments to finish, lectures to slog through, part-time jobs and pressure, pressure, pressure! But hey, it's Christmas! There's a party every night and a million distractions in the shape of eligible men. Marina and Rob are getting serious, Sinead and Travis are on again big time, then off again, then on... But it's fun-time Frankie who's hitting the headlines – getting herself work as a model and finally landing herself a man!

Wim is tall, Dutch and a juggler with an alternative circus group. Pity he's also Mr Unreliable, with a string of girlfriends, as Sinead and Marina quickly discover. The big question is – should they tell Frankie that Wim juggles women too? Or should they let her enjoy the few scraps of pleasure he throws her way? The girls make the mistake of telling, and suddenly Frankie isn't smiling any more...

ISBN 1-416-90105-1